BANNON'S
LAW

I

THE STRANGER

Beyond the upthrust rind of the farthest horizon the sun rose straight into a flawless pale sky, pouring brilliance and springtime warmth as light and soft as polished gold down across the world which ran southward, as well as easterly and westerly, from Dennison.

The lad riding his pudding-footed old grey horse came down across the open country to the north-west, heading towards the coachroad, and when he passed between that pair of smelly juniper trees folks called The Twins, he twisted to peer northward because if there was a stage coming he'd hang back and let it pass first.

He wasn't riding a green colt so it wasn't that he expected the grey horse to shy out from under him at the sight and noise of a hastening stagecoach. It was rather that he was by nature diffident; he was a squatter's kid of fifteen and for the past five years he had been learning that while folks were created equal, for a plain fact some were a lot more equal than others, and the least equal of them all, even less equal than the redskins around the Dennison cow country, were homesteaders like his folks—and like he was, although he was not a squatter's son by choice, just by circumstance.

The grey horse plodded steadily along. He hadn't had a single cup in his teeth for at least seven years and although the lad's father continued to say the old horse was nine, which was when he'd first got smooth-mouthed, for a fact he was a lot closer to twenty, and it showed up in those sunken places above his eyes, in the flatness of his chin, and in other ways as well. But they took good care of him. Not because they were especially fond of the horse but because he was one of a team of greys they owned, and they had no money to replace either grey if anything happened to them, and there was no way under the sun to survive as a home-steader unless there was a team to do the hard work when it came time to put in a crop.

Even then, there were no guarantees about surviving.

The old horse knew every yard of the trail from the home-stead to the cow-town of Dennison. He had walked between those two juniper trees at least a hundred times over the past five years, and he did it now with his head low, his eyes fixed dully and without interest on the yonder roadway, then he caught an unsettling scent, turned to trace it out, and without warning suddenly gave a tremendous shy side-ways, landing stiff-legged and with his back bowed.

The boy went off and struck the ground before the horse had stopped moving. He was looking up the road but even if he hadn't been he was bareback and completely unsus-pecting so he would have gone off anyway.

He rolled when he landed and came up onto his feet with the instinctive reaction of a boy who had gone off horses before—many times. He was not hurt at all, but he

6

was jarred and he was also angered.

He swore at the old horse and picked up a rock to hurl, then turned very slowly to follow out the direction the old horse was staring, still bunched up, still with a bow to his neck as though he were going to snort, and still with his dull eyes sprung wide and looking glassy.

There was a man seated in the shade of one of the old junipers. He was paying absolutely no attention to the lad and the grey horse. He hadn't even turned his head in fact when the commotion had erupted.

He was sitting with both shoulders planted against the scaly bark of the tree-trunk, his legs thrust out in front, and both hands in his lap. He had grey in the unshorn hair around his ears, his face was lined and bronzed from long exposure, and he looked asleep except that his eyes were open.

He was wearing an ivory-handled Colt in a shiny old russet holster. His shellbelt was about two-thirds full of cartridges. His boots were worn and he had silver-mounted spurs on each boot. His hat was lying at his side, evidently where he had dropped it when he had sat down in the shade to rest.

And he was dead.

The boy had hair beginning to bristle along the back of his neck. Realisation came slowly, but it eventually arrived, and although the lad could see no marks of violence, although there was no visible blood nor bruises, the boy could sense death.

After a moment he walked gingerly around in front of the seated man, stopped poised for immediate flight, and tried to meet the man's stare. But there was nothing to meet; the man's eyes were open but had that unique complete blankness only found in the eyes of the dead.

As time passed the youth's astonishment and fear atrophied. He looked for the man's horse. Not only was the man a rangerider, by his attire, but no one walked out here, even if they came from a place as nearby as Dennison.

There were shod-horse imprints around the juniper and they seemed to go south-westerly, but there was no view of the horse, so the youth logically concluded this man had died hours earlier; maybe even last night for all anyone knew, and his horse had had that much time to wander off.

Someone would find the horse, of course. Saddled and bridled, but riderless, horses were always found and taken to town to the sheriff or were taken to some nearby cow-outfit and held there.

The boy had never owned a horse, even in this territory where mustangs and off-breeds were a dollar or two a head. He had never had a dollar or two either. There were a lot of things the squatter-lad had never had.

He eyed the handsomely silver inlaid rangerider spurs on the corpse, and that ivory-butted sixgun. There really was nothing to prevent him from taking one of those items, or even both of them, any more than there was anything to prevent him from plundering the pockets of the dead man. He was bound to have money. You could tell by looking at them which ones had it and which ones did not have it. This one had it.

Finally, the grey horse recovered, decided that seated individual in juniper-shade was no threat after all, and dropped his head to go nosing left and right for some browse. It was this action which drove the lad to his reluctant conclusion. He did not touch the corpse, did not even go close enough to minutely examine those elegant spurs, but turned, caught the grey horse, looked around for a rock or a stump to use in mounting, found nothing suitable and stepped back, caught hold of the old horse's tail, used each hock as a foothold and climbed up, scooted over the rump to the back and leaned over the neck with both hands to catch hold of dragging reins.

He looked back three times before reaching the coach-road. Back there, nothing had changed. He looked again in all directions for the dead man's horse. Nothing had changed about that either—there was no horse in sight.

Dennison looked alive and busy, on southward. There was a little skiff of dun dust rising over the town to the southward, down near the lower end of town where the smithy, the livery barn and the public corrals were.

It did not happen every day, nor even every week, but occasionally horsetraders or mustangers came into Dennison and took over the public corrals. Sometimes there were unannounced auctions but more often the traders first put on an impromptu rodeo to attract folks, *then* tried to peddle their horses.

That was probably what the dust was all about.

Otherwise, the town looked as it usually appeared; flourishing and busy, and a little noisy. It had always fascinated the squatter's son even though he knew perfectly well how the townsmen, the rangemen and even the merchants felt about settlers, including the urchins belonging to settlers, and he was also very prudent while in town although as yet he had developed no feeling of resentment. That might come later, when he was older. Right now when he entered town from the north, with a note in his pocket for Abe Markham, the big, bearded proprietor of the general store, he was wide-eyed with interest. At fifteen he could imagine no finer nor exciting way of life than being a town-kid.

The sheriff's office and jailhouse were in the same log building on the west side of the main thoroughfare, mid-way along. That structure like some other structures around town had once been part of the inner compound, a generation back, when there had been no town and the place had been called Fort Dennison. In those days the inhabitants had been soldiers, their civilian scouts, packers, suttlers and whatnot. Nowadays there was not a soldier within a hundred miles, the palisaded walls had come down long ago, and 'Fort' had been dropped from the name. Now, it was just plain Dennison, New Mexico Territory.

The youth turned in at the tie-rack out front of the jail-house building under the indifferent gaze of some passers-by, and the snickers of two town youths who whispered back and forth about the barefoot, raggedy-pantsed squatter-kid astride his ugly old grey horse without a saddle.

A lean, weathered, greying man came forth and halted to stare out at the youth in front of the tie-rack. He had a sweat-stained dark brown hat, a tied-down Colt and a dull small badge on his shirtfront. He and the squatter-boy eyed one another for a moment, then the youth said, " Mister, are you the sheriff?"

"Yeah," replied the man. " You're a settler's kid and you've come to tell me some cowmen ran off your milk cow."

" No, sir. I come to tell you there's a dead feller sitting under one of them juniper trees north of town on the west side of the stageroad. Just sitting there."

2

POCHO

Sheriff Tom Cartland was a former rangerider. In fact it had been said of Tom Cartland that if he'd taken to the law enforcement profession earlier in his lifetime he might have made a better peace officer. But that was not a unanimous view, and in fact when he hiked on up to Doctor Bannon's cottage, which was a combination clinic in front and living quarters out back, he went in search of a man in Dennison who had consistently approved of Sheriff Cartland's variety of—sometimes unorthodox—law enforcement.

Maybe that was because Doctor Bannon was in his own way a trifle unorthodox, also. He was, like Abe Markham, a widower. But after that Joshua Bannon's similarity to anyone else in town ended. He had been an army physician and he had also practised medicine in some large eastern city. He was unyielding in his oppositions, forthright in his outspoken opinions—sometimes needlessly so—and he seemed to always smell of cigar smoke and carbolic acid—or some kind of medicine.

He was out back in the vegetable patch when the sheriff came down the south side of the cottage and found him. It was a delightful springtime morning, not too hot and not chilly at all. A perfect time to weed the corn and squash.

He looked up, straightened back and fished forth a hand-kerchief to mop a pale brow with, then said, " Good morning, Tom. Let me guess—some blasted settler's woman miscarried last night."

Sheriff Cartland swept a low glance over the neat, orderly, weeded rows of the doctor's garden. " A settler's kid came into town a half-hour ago and reported a dead man up at the Twin Junipers. I sent a feller up from the livery barn with a wagon to fetch the corpse down here to you. Figured I'd ought to tell you."

Joshua Bannon turned to step into some house-shade as he said, " That's thoughtful of you. Well, what am I supposed to do—pump him full of salt water and clean him up for burying?"

Cartland nodded. " I expect. At least get him ready, Doc. I'll come along this afternoon and look at him. If he's known we'll send word to someone to come get him. If he isn't known we'll do like always—appropriate his gatherings and auction them off to pay for the burying."

Sheriff Cartland's brows pulled inwards and downward. " No horse nor saddle."

" Any blood?" asked Doctor Bannon. " If not maybe he had a heart seizure and toppled off, in which case the horse would have been free to run off. Well, no matter, when they put him in the carriage shed out back I'll look at him . . . By the way, Tom, I got green peppers almost ready to eat. You like green peppers, do you?"

Sheriff Cartland looked pained. " I don't like any kind of

peppers, Doc, to be downright truthful with you, and living in New Mexico hasn't changed that one darned bit. I never saw so many folks can't make a decent meal without grinding up peppers into everything."

" They keep a man from having worms," stated Doctor Bannon. " They are a good tonic for thinnin' the blood, especially at this time of the year."

Sheriff Cartland sighed, looked among the rows until he saw the little flourishing pepper plants. " I do appreciate the offer. Anyway, bein' an unmarried man I don't have any way to cook them."

" That's something else you'd ought to give some thought to, Tom. It's not natural for a feller no older than you are to spend his life between a rooming-house and a jailhouse-office."

Tom Cartland looked down his nose. " I'll be back later to look at the corpse. Don't want to keep you from weedin' those gawddamned peppers, Doc."

Sheriff Cartland returned to the roadway and headed in a bee-line for the livery barn at the lower end of town. It still bothered him that the dead man had not had a horse standing by. But, of course, as Doc had pointed out, if the man had just collapsed very suddenly . . .

The liveryman was a thin, slightly stooped man with very close-spaced pale eyes and a bad set of brown teeth. His attitude was of a man who was always listening for something; he even carried his head a little to one side.

His name was Brutus Tolbert. People who had known him for any length of time made no comments on his first name. Those who did not know him at all, made no comments either. More as a result of cautious frontier policy than good manners. But everyone who came into contact with Tolbert was entitled to wonder what a man's folks had been thinking of to hang that handle on a child. It was common knowledge, even west of the Missouri, that historically someone named Brutus had not been on a footing with Abe Lincoln or General Grant.

Maybe that was why the liveryman carried his head a little to one side. Maybe he expected someone to make a derogatory remark and he wanted to be sure to hear it the first time. In any case when Sheriff Cartland got down there and asked about a stray horse wearing a bridle and saddle, being brought in, Brutus Tolbert shook his head.

"What is it this time? Some greenhorn got off to step behind a tree and forgot to tie his animal?"

"Under a tree, Brutus, not behind it. Well, maybe some cow-outfit found the horse," stated Cartland, and turned as Abe Markham's wispy store-clerk came up looking troubled. He was an old man, thin and wiry and waspish. He'd been a clerk at Markham's general store since the day of Abe's father. His name was Amos Jennings and although he had never married—as far as folks knew anyway—it was rumoured that in his profligate youth as a scout and freighter for the army he'd begot several half-Arapahoe pups. But that could have been plain spite; old Amos was not a well-liked man.

He ignored Brutus Tolbert and skewered Tom Cartland with his chilly blue stare as he said, "There's a confounded drunk beneath the loading dock out back, Sheriff, and we can't get the team and wagon backed up to load it because every time we try it that bastard under there sets up a caterwauling and it spooks the horses."

Brutus, with his head slightly to one side, looked caustically at the older man. "Why'n't you just crawl under there and yank him out, instead of huntin' up the sheriff? It's only one drunk, ain't it?"

Amos stiffened and refused to even glance in Tolbert's direction. "Thing is, Sheriff, Mister Markham asked me to find you and get you to get him out from unner there. I got to go back now, so what should I tell Mister Markham?"

Cartland eyed Jennings, whom he had known ever since he'd been in the Dennison territory, and whom he had never been able to work up any feeling for, one way or the other. "Let's go," he muttered, and turned once more towards the liveryman. "Brutus, if anyone fetches in a stray horse with a saddle and . . ."

"I know, Sheriff, I know. I'll hunt you up right away."

Amos walked erectly away from the livery barn, stalked diagonally across the roadway in the direction of the narrow dog-trot between the general store building and the harness shop next door, and paused at the entrance of the narrow passageway to say, "I'm not a guessing man, Sheriff. But if I was, I'd guess the drunk is that Mex or half-Mex, whatever he is, that works for Jim Bryan over at the stage company's corralyard. He sounds like a Messican."

Cartland gestured for his companion to lead off down through the dog-trot and when they emerged out back

Markham's wagon and its nice big sorrel team was parked out a few yards where it blocked the alleyway. The horses were craning their heads around as far as a check-rein would allow, peering at the dark area beneath the battered old log-loading dock.

Amos Jennings stopped, pointed and said, " There. Fling a stone under there and he'll groan at you."

Sheriff Cartland complied. No sooner had the stone tumbled beneath the dock than a man groaned in a wavery tone. Cartland looked sceptically at Amos. " You can tell he's a Messican just from that?"

" It's the accent. Or don't you have that fine an ear?"

Tom Cartland did not reply but his final glance was withering, then he stepped over, put his hat atop the dock and dropped to his knees.

" Pocho! Is that you under there? This here is Sheriff Cartland. Shag your butt out here and don't fool around."

Instead of obedience, Sheriff Cartland got another of those groaning moans, so he started crawling. The earth under there was clammy, moist and crumbly and the place smelled of debris and staleness.

By the time Cartland could see the drunk he was two-thirds of the way towards the rear-wall footing of the store building and it was hopelessly dark.

He stopped, tried to make out a face instead of just a lump of man-shape under there, and spoke in Spanish this time. " Look you, man, crawl out from beneath here before I drag you out by the hair!"

This time the drunk leaned, looked long and hard, then

17

replied in Spanish. " Be tranquil, chief, I'm coming out."

Jennings had been correct, it was the cock-eyed, pock-marked, overweight, mahogany-coloured hostler from the corralyard. The man known as Pocho—which was not really a name, it was a slang term for anyone who lived along the border and who did everything like a half-gringo, half-beaner. In this instance, though, it was a name. Perhaps because no one had ever bothered to discover Pocho's real name. Or maybe they had bothered and had turned up something unpronounceable. In any case, Pocho worked; the hostler answered to it, and as he started bear-crawling past Sheriff Cartland now, he turned a shiny, soiled face and grinned. There was little visible except a set of very large, very white teeth.

" You thought I was drunk," said Pocho. " You would lock me up for being drunk, *amigo*, but you can see I am not drunk at all." Pocho crawled almost to the lighted end of the dock, then simply rocked over and fell on his face flat on the ground. Then he groaned again.

Amos Jennings stepped up, bent a trifle gingerly to peer at the downed man, then made a sniffing sound. " I knew it. I knew it all the time. Sheriff, where are you?"

Cartland crawled out, stood up knocking dirt off his hands and knees. He avoided Jennings's glance and picked up his hat. " Get up," he growled at the prone Mexican. " Pocho, darn your hide get up out of there."

Amos said, " He's passed out. Good lord, I can smell his breath all the way up here. He's drunk as a skunk, Sheriff."

" Don't Mister Markham need you inside, Amos?"

18

Jennings acted deaf. "What do you figure to do with him? He'd ought to be locked up and dried out."

"You want to help me drag him over to the jailhouse?"

"I wouldn't lay a finger on him in that condition!"

"Then gawddammit go on inside the store and shut up," growled the annoyed lawman, crushing his old hat down atop his head, then leaning to catch hold of the Mexican's shoulder to lean back and haul Pocho upright.

But the hostler was a heavier man than he looked to be. It took both hands and just about all the physical strength Sheriff Cartland had to hoist Pocho up and lean him against the loading dock.

Amos made a derisive snort and stamped up the steps and across the dock and inside. He slammed the dock-door after himself.

That resounding noise brought Pocho around. He even acted as though he would drop to the ground and try to crawl but Tom Cartland held him in an iron, two-fisted grip and said, "It was just a door slamming. Pocho, I'd ought to kick your rear all the way over to the jailhouse and lock you up for a month."

That too had an awakening effect. Pocho looked anxiously from muddy eyes. "*Jefe,* we are short-handed at the yard!"

"What in the hell were you doing under Markham's dock; why didn't you just bed down in the corralyard bunkhouse if you had to get drunk?"

Pocho pulled free of the supporting hands and steadied himself as he replied. "Mister Bryan will fire anyone who

19

gets drunk around the yard or the office."

"But why under here?"

"Listen, *jefe*, we're old friends. Tom Cartland and Pocho. I'll tell you . . . There is a girl named Jesusita, and she has a terrible old mother. Well, the old mother was looking for me last night. *Jefe*, maybe she had a gun, no?"

"Why would she . . . Pocho, what did you do to the girl?"

The burly, squaty very dark man rolled his good eye and the cocked one came around in its own time. "Nothing. I swear to you. Nothing at all." Pocho sighed loudly. "I give you my word, I didn't do it. I only tried. For that the old *señora* wants to shoot me, or maybe take a knife and slit my . . ."

"Pocho, you go on over to the corralyard. If there is likely to be trouble between you and the girl's mother, you tell Jim Bryan."

Pocho's eyes rolled again, not in unison, never in unison. "I can't tell Mister Bryan, *jefe*. He'll fire me."

"What kind of a choice do you have, Pocho? You tell Jim and he can maybe send you out to the horse-pasture ranch for a few weeks, or you can hang around and that old lady's going to shoot you . . . Now listen to me; take your darned troubles somewhere else. And don't crawl under Markham's dock any more when you get drunk. Now go on over to the yard."

"You're not going to lock me up?"

Tom Cartland eyed the stocky man with an unsmiling gaze. "Why should I lock you up? If you're out free maybe the old lady'll shoot you then I won't have any more trouble from you." Cartland turned, stalked up the steps and went into the store where Abe Markham and his wispy old clerk were talking. When they saw the sheriff they turned and waited until he approached.

Amos Jennings said, " I was telling Mister Markham . . ."

Cartland did not look gratified about that, he shrugged it off and addressed the store's proprietor with whom he had been on good terms for some years now.

" Some Mex woman is after him for monkeying around with her daughter, Abe, and I sent him over to the corral-yard to get over his drunk in his own territory."

Markham nodded but his clerk was incensed. " You didn't lock him up? The law says you got to lock up troublesome drunks. That's how it's always been here in Dennison. Since the sheriff before you, and the sheriff before him."

Abe Markham saw the lawman's neck reddening so he pointed towards the front of the store. " There's a customer up yonder, Amos."

As the clerk departed looking as vinegary as usual, Tom Cartland let his breath out slowly. " He's a regular old cranky granny."

Abe Markham agreed without equivocation. " And worse'n that, even. But he's one hell of a good store-clerk, Tom. Come on in the office, I got a new case of Scotch whisky in there. Just off the freight wagon out of Council Bluffs."

It was too early in the day. " Maybe later, or another

time," stated Sheriff Cartland. " I got to get up to Doc's place."

" Well, thanks for getting Jim Bryan's Messican out from under the loading-dock, Tom."

Cartland forced a thin smile and walked on through and out the front door.

3

IDENTIFICATION OF A DEAD MAN

Doctor Bannon had his hat on, his coat off, his sleeves rolled up and was lighting a cigar in his office when the sheriff walked into the waiting-room and called out. Doc puffed up a healthy fire before singing out for Cartland to enter the office, and afterwards, with Tom Cartland in there with him, Doc pointed to a chair, until he was satisfied his cigar was properly lighted. Unless they were lighted all around they tended to burn unevenly.

Sheriff Cartland did not smoke. Hadn't smoked in about twelve years, and although the scent of smoke did not ordinarily bother him he could not abide the aroma of Joshua Bannon's stogies. They were black, thin, and crooked, came up out of Mexico when the freighters passed through heading north, and were cheap. A safe assumption would be that the price appealed most to Doctor Bannon, who was a very penurious individual.

Tom Cartland went over, hoisted a closed window a few inches and remained over there while he said, " Did the body get down here?"

Bannon nodded, plugged the cigar between worn teeth and looked serenely upwards. " He's out back in the embalmin' shed. If you want his clothing, it's on a nail out there. But you'll not get much from that. The pockets were as empty as last year's bird-nest."

Cartland scowled. " Nothing at all?"

" Some matches, a sack of tobacco with a packet of papers. A Barlow clasp-knife and that is all." Doc removed the cigar. " And he didn't die of a heart seizure the way we figured. He's been shot in the back." Doc shoved the stogie back between his teeth, leaned back and clasped both hands behind his head. " I'd guess he'd been shot maybe three or four days. It was a small-calibre slug. It's on a dish out there on the table beside the corpse, if you want it. I'd also guess he wasn't shot up close otherwise that bullet would probably have come out in front. It didn't. It was lodged inside him, and I dug it out neat as a whistle. He had haemorrhaged and when he got off the horse he was feeling very weak. Probably very drowsy too. So he sat down—and that is where he died, bled out internally."

Tom Cartland forgot about the objectionable cigar smoke. But he was not particularly upset over the situation arising from the condition of that stranger's corpse. After all, this was springtime, the time of year when all the range country from Arizona to Montana had scores of rangemen passing through in search of work, and every year there were some of those cowboys who just never made it back home again. Of course, it was different when one died of a bullet wound instead of beneath the hooves of frightened cattle, or as a result of being stood on his head in a pile of granite boulders by some vicious saddlehorse. But there was just so much a peace officer could do. Tom Cartland, for example, did not feel especially obligated; he would do everything he knew how to do in order to identify the cowboy and to afterwards notify his next of kin—if he had any—but unless the man had been carrying some kind of identification, Tom probably would simply have to supervise at the burial of another John Doe rangerider. It would not be the first one planted at the Dennison cemetery and probably would not be the last one.

Under Doc's cynical gaze, through bluish smoke, Sheriff Cartland shrugged. "It's springtime all right. They're riding up every lousy canyon from here to there and back again."

Doc seemed disinclined to be that philosophical. "But this man died as a result of being shot," he said, removing the cigar. "It's not the same as being killed by a bucking horse, is it?"

"You said there was nothing in his pockets to identify him with, Doc. Where does that leave us? With an unknown dead man on our hands. So, we do the best we can, and we plant him out yonder."

Doc considered the tip of his stogie. "This one's different, sonny," he murmured, and raised his tough, shrewd glance to Cartland again. He leaned, pulled something from a drawer and pitched it at Cartland without warning. "You know what that is? It's a moneybelt. Look inside it and tell me this was just some unlucky cowboy riding through who happened to die here. You don't have to count it, I've already done that. There is six thousand dollars in U.S. greenbacks in that belt."

Cartland left the window, sat down and unlashed the belt's inner compartments. Someone had very neatly and meticulously folded notes of large denomination until they fitted perfectly without making a single bulge.

And Doctor Bannon was right, there was six thousand dollars in those doe-skin compartments.

Tom raised his head to meet the steady, cynical stare of Joshua Bannon. Doc smiled a little but with a downward pull at the corners of his mouth. " All you got to do is find out who he was, then find out where he'd been, and after that all you got to do is find which bank he robbed, which bullion coach he stopped, or which ranch-family he murdered to get all that cash . . . Just another cowboy ridin' through, eh?"

Sheriff Cartland did not say a thing. He began putting the money back with as much care as the original owner of the belt had done. It gave him a little time, and right now that was what he needed. He had never in his life encountered six thousand dollars in cash before. He'd seen a few large notes and cheques, but never that much actual cash money.

As he fastened the final compartment in the belt he said, " Well, let's go out back and look at him, and at his clothes."

Doc was willing, but as he led the way out through the kitchen into the yard beyond, out the picket-gate back there and across the alley to his old carriage-house which had not housed a horse, nor even a buggy in ten years, he said, " You're not going to find anything," and he was correct.

26

There was nothing outstanding in the appearance of the corpse. The man was bronzed from the throat up, and from the throat down he was as grey-white-pale as a snail. Tom had not expected the body to tell him anything anyway, but what began to bother him, was that by the time he had finished a minute examination of the clothing, the boots, even the holster and gunbelt, he did not know anything either. There was usually a name of a harness-maker inside a shellbelt, or the name of a bootmaker inside a boot. This man actually did not have a single thing which could have been used to back-track him, and as Tom Cartland dropped the last boot and lifted out the sixgun to turn it over and over, he said, "Doc, it isn't possible not to have some kind of name, somewhere."

Bannon had had more time to consider this phenomenon and he had arrived at some conclusions, one of which he offered now.

"There is, Tom, if you just sat yourself down and went through everything you owned and removed all names of folks and of towns." Bannon picked up the shellbelt and turned it inside out. "Right there where that leather's been scraped, used to be a name of a maker and his town." He dropped the shellbelt. "There's one source left—this feller's horse and saddle, and maybe his saddlebags and blanketroll —if he had 'em on his saddle." Doc smiled pithily. "Where are they?"

Cartland turned his back on the corpse shaking his head. "If they're around I'll find them," he answered. "And if there's been a recent robbery where someone got off with loot in the amount of six thousand dollars, that hadn't ought to be too hard to find out either."

"And," said Doc, "got off with a bullet in his back." Doc looked past at the face of the dead man. "It's discouragin' to be in my business at times. Look there; in his forties I'd guess, with another fifteen, twenty years ahead. I wish I had those years ahead of me. And what did he sell them for—thirty pieces of silver in the form of six thousand in greenbacks. A miserable bargain, Tom."

Cartland did not even glance around. The man was dead, and in dying he had saddled Sheriff Cartland with a responsibility Tom Cartland did not appreciate. His personal feeling towards the corpse was one of antagonism—but it was pointless to be angry at something which was dead.

Tom crossed to the doorway and took down the dead man's clothing, picked up his spurred boots and draped the gun and shellbelt over one arm, then he reached to let himself out into the alley again.

Doc trooped back through the house, again leading the way, and when they were in the reception room out front—which Doc called his "vestibule"—Cartland said, "Whoever shot him sure as hell knew he had this money. Either as a former owner of the money, or maybe as a gunguard on a stagecoach or a teller in a bank."

Doc tried to puff life back into his cold cigar and failed, so he shoved it to one side of his mouth and spoke around it. "And they'll be looking for him—well—for the six thousand anyway."

Cartland nodded. "Right. Next question is : Would they

know he'd come down here to the Dennison country, and if they knew it, will they show up looking for him?"

Doc was sanguine about that. " I hope not. I'm a medical practitioner not a gunfighter. I don't want to have a lot of trouble over this man, too. That's your department, not mine."

Sheriff Cartland was mildly puzzled. " Why should you have trouble?"

" Because every place I've ever been, sonny, dead folks are sent to the doctor or the undertaker, and in a place like Dennison the doctor *is* the undertaker—and I'd be the first one to undress the corpse, wouldn't I? The first to find that moneybelt."

Cartland nodded and departed carrying the unidentified dead man's attire down to his spurred boots and the gun and shellbelt. Doctor Bannon stood on the porch gazing after him.

It was still fairly early in the day. After Cartland carefully stowed the corpse's affects in his cupboard at the office he went back down to the livery barn, but this time when Brutus Tolbert saw him approaching he began wagging his head to indicate there still had been no stray horse show up, Tom Cartland had something else on his mind.

" Strangers," he said to Tolbert. " Maybe one, maybe two or three of them, Brutus, maybe not rangeriders, but asking around and . . ."

" Askin' around about what?" Tolbert enquired, dropping his head to one side. " Just what'n'ell are you leading up to, Sheriff? That dead feller they delivered to Doc's shed?"

"Yeah. Him." Tom Cartland did not want to make a confidant of Tolbert but he had been pretty well manoeuvred into a corner. Also, if the arrival of the unknown dead man in Dennison was not now generally known, it *would* be common knowledge within a few hours. Dennison was one of those towns; the only really successful secrets were the ones someone told first, before they were ferreted out.

But Sheriff Cartland did not confide anything in Brutus beyond the death of the stranger, and when he admitted there was no clue as to the dead man's identity, he could see the little closed-spaced eyes of Tolbert brightening with their sly, crafty expression.

"He didn't have nothing at all with a name on it, Sheriff?"

Instead of offering a direct retort Sheriff Cartland said, "That's why I need his horse and outfit. At least the horse will be branded."

Brutus grew pensive and pursued his thin lips. "I tell you what I'll do," he said. "I'll ask everyone who comes in for the next few days. From the outlying ranches, and the freighters, and everyone I run onto. That had ought to turn up something, Sheriff."

Tom Cartland smiled, agreed that it might indeed turn up something, and departed heading northward in the direction of his office, not satisfied that Tolbert's enquiries would turn up a blessed thing, because it was also quite possible that if someone who needed a saddle animal, already rigged out and ready to use such as some of the raggedy-pantsed squatters around the territory, came onto that loose horse, neither Brutus Tolbert nor anyone else would find out what had happened to the beast for a long while—if they *ever* found out.

He went out into the small closet-like storeroom off the sheriff's office and lit the smoky lamp back there to spend a half-hour pawing through musty—and very dusty—boxes of old wanted dodgers.

Among the older posters he sought a face. Among the much more recent ones he sought mention of a six thousand dollar robbery, and what he came up with after an interminable search, was nothing.

Among printed descriptions he could have pulled at least two dozen handbills listing men who could have answered the dead man's description : six feet tall, about one hundred and seventy pounds, about forty or thereabouts, sandy hair with a touch of grey above the ears, blue eyes, occupation cowboy, rangeman, hostler.

He went back out front, poked in the firebox of the little cast-iron office stove to make some red coals appear, and he pitched in two handfuls of kindling, then slammed the door and set his granite-ware coffeepot atop the stove's solitary burner, and went over to the roadway window and lean and thoughtfully gaze out.

He had locked the moneybelt with its contents in the ugly little grey iron safe bolted to the floor behind his desk, and as he eventually turned to look over where the coffee was beginning to send forth a delightful aroma, his glance lingered for a time upon the little safe.

It occurred to him that whoever had been in pursuit of the dead man—assuming that anyone at all had been after him, which seemed to be a reasonable assumption—if they traced him to Dennison, which was also a reasonable thing to assume, and if they heard about an unidentified dead man being buried in Dennison—they were going to know damned well that someone around town had that laden moneybelt.

What would a searcher's immediate concern be? To find where the moneybelt was being held, naturally, and that would clearly be either in someone's safe, or in someone like the sheriff of Dennison County's personal care. As bait, perhaps his little iron office safe was worthwhile. Also, he could himself be a worthwhile magnet for someone, but he preferred to think it might be the safe. For an obvious reason he did not want to be stalked by someone he did not know, had never seen and could not predict.

He went back, got a cup of coffee, and stood for a long while in private thought. His conclusions were built around what seemed an inevitable event. He would eventually be able to identify the corpse because someone who had known that dead man was certainly going to arrive in Dennison.

In fact the longer he stood there sipping black java the more it occurred to him that the identity of the corpse was most probably going to become a factor of secondary interest—one which he would ultimately discover as the result of either finding someone who had known the dead man, or being accosted by someone who was searching for *him*.

4

CARTLAND'S HUNCH

They buried that John Doe cowboy shortly after four o'clock in the afternoon two days after his discovery out under the Twin Pines. Doctor Bannon was there along with Sheriff Cartland and the Methodist minister, a bushy-headed man with eyes so close-set they were ferret-like, and a glib way of making his eulogy sound as though the un-identified cowboy, or outlaw, or whatever he had been, was a long-time personal acquaintance, and when it was over with the diggers moving in discreetly to get the hole filled before suppertime, Tom Cartland strolled back towards town beside Doc and said, " I hope to hell I don't get that preacher to speak over my grave."

Doc shrugged. " What's the difference; you won't hear him." Doc found the cigar he'd been rummaging inside his coat for. " Where is the moneybelt?"

" In my office-safe."

" Abe Markham's safe's better over at the general store. That little iron box of yours can be dynamited."

" Any safe can be dynamited, Doc, it depends on how much explosive they use," stated Cartland. " And because I know Abe, I know he'd have a fit if I put that moneybelt in his safe without explaining someone might come along and try to get at it. And he'd refuse to let me put the thing in his safe if I told him the truth."

Doc got the evil little Mex stogie lighted. As he cast aside the sulphur match he dryly said, " You certainly do have your problems, don't you?"

Tom ignored the sarcasm. When they reached the plank-walk and stepped up onto it out of the dust of back-road byways Tom said, " That darned horse . . ."

" No sign of him yet?"

" No, and it's been three days." Tom turned southward alongside Doctor Bannon. " If he don't turn up today I'm going to have to start riding out and around, asking and looking."

Bannon was not particularly concerned. " Just remember if you find him that someone, the town or someone anyway, owes me five dollars for posting the corpse and for laying him out to be buried. Say, what about his gun and spurs. They looked pretty handsome to me for some brush-popper to be wearing."

Tom paused at the picket gate out front of Doctor Bannon's cottage and looked disapprovingly down his nose. " You'll get paid," he said, and walked briskly on down to the jailhouse office.

Brutus Tolbert was sitting on a wall-bench tipped so far back his feet were off the floor. He could have been sitting there for an hour or more and he looked completely relaxed and in no hurry to move, not even when the lawman entered, shot him a look as he pitched aside his hat and tugged off the black shoe-string necktie.

Brutus watched the black tie come off. " Got him buried, did you? For a fact, Sheriff, whenever I see you wearin' that little black tie I get uneasy."

Tom went behind the table to scratch, then to sit down. " He's planted. As for the black tie—you got to show some respect for them even when you don't have any idea who they are—who they *were*. Well, you got the loose horse, Brutus?"

Tolbert's ferret-eyes narrowed. " That was a fair guess," he mumbled. " Nope, I don't have him, but like I told you, I'd keep nosin' around, askin' folks when they come to the barn, and all like that."

" And?"

" And there's a pedlar who come into town early this morning on his way south towards Beaverton, said some squatter tried to sell him a fine buckskin horse, saddle bridle, blanket and all, only yesterday."

" Where?"

Brutus unconsciously gestured. " North-west, up the stageroad, and over along the foothills a mile or two where the pedlar come down a game-trail." Brutus let his arm drop. " You know that settler-country very well, do you? Well, I sure do. I been hunting up my stray horses out through there for five years now. I know exactly the place where this settler tried to peddle the buckskin horse." Brutus dropped his head more and more to one side. " You want me to ride up there with you? I know exactly the place."

Tom Cartland did not want to spend the balance of the

35

day in Tolbert's company. Furthermore, he knew those foothills probably as well as did Brutus because he had been hunting up through there every autumn. He said, " I'll find the settler," and thanked Tolbert for coming in with that information.

After the liveryman departed Cartland went out back to the shed and corrals across the alley, got his black horse, left the bay behind and after rigging out he rode up the alleyway.

The foothills actually were not distant, but when a man struck out late in the afternoon there was no possibility of him getting up there, finding a sodbuster with a buckskin saddle-animal, and getting back again until it was very late.

Brutus would have protested. Most of the people around town would in fact have protested about doing something so late in the day which ordinarily should have been done early in the morning.

Tom Cartland had a method about things of this nature. When he went man-hunting across open range country where he was visible—and recognisable—for miles in advance of his arrival, and he did not want to be detected, he simply waited until late afternoon and struck out, ensuring in this fashion that by the time he arrived in a locality he wanted to visit it would be so dark watchers—if there were any—would be unable to discern him.

Settlers were a motley, devious, sly bunch. Maybe hardship and circumstances had made them that way and maybe that was not their fault, but Sheriff Cartland was a law officer not a sociologist, he cared about people—squatters or anyone else—breaking the law, and he cared about detecting them at it, or catching them afterwards. In this instance he was particularly concerned because he was genuinely interested in finding out the identity of that dead man they had buried earlier in the day. And the original source of all that money.

He rode north-westerly from town, boosting his horse over into a gentle little rocking-chair lope which was easy on horse and rider, and which the beast could keep up for an hour or more without tiring.

He knew the game-trail the pedlar had used to come down out of the northward mountains parallel to the coach-road. There were any number of game-trails up through there but there was only one which made the complete crossing from the plateau-country north of the Dennison Mountains, down across the rim and on over into the countryside around Dennison. In fact, it was more an old trapper-trail than a game-trail, but if folks wanted to call it a game-trail it was perfectly agreeable with Tom Cartland.

He was not especially interested in the trail anyway, except insofar as it enabled him to pinpoint the locality where someone had tried to peddle a buckskin riding horse, and even that might not have meant a whole lot except that he happened to know that most of those hard-scrabble settlers up through that foothill country on the south end of the old trapper-trail were as poor as church mice. If any of them had ever owned a decent saddle-horse he would have peddled it long ago, or would at least have traded it

37

down around Dennison for flour and baking soda, sugar and salt.

And that lad who had found the dead man was the off-spring of a homesteader directly below the base of the old trapper-trail. The name of that particular clan of squatters was O'Grady.

It did not have to mean much that the O'Gradys were involved to the extent at least of being the first to find that dead man, and that now they were directly ahead at the base of the settler's access-trail to the back-country. Coincidences fill the world. For all Sheriff Cartland knew—or cared—they might fill the entire universe.

But if that dead outlaw, or whatever he was, had been riding a buckskin horse, then it was going to be stretching the credibility of a coincidence right out to its darned limits to find the horse at O'Grady's corral.

Cartland hauled his black down to a walk when he knew he was only a few miles out, loosened the reins so his horse could drop its head and plod onward, studied the gloomy heavens and breathed deeply in appreciation of springtime, even in the evening. He did not believe there would be springtime nights—or early summertime nights as well—anywhere on earth to match these of New Mexico. Then a dog barked ahead somewhere through the settling darkness and he came back down to hard reality with a quiet curse, turned the horse slightly to pass out and around the first sordid collection of sheds and shacks where a squatter resided, and began an encircling sashay so that he could be in behind the lower homesteads, hopefully with the wind—

such as there was of it—coming up-country to carry his scent rearward rather than southward down where the homesteaders—and their dogs—lived.

Someone had once said in Barney Shannon's saloon down at Dennison that settlers were like prairie-dogs; they all hunched up together and lived in sordid closeness, maybe for protection but more likely because they were afraid of just about everything and needed one another to lean on all the time. It was not a bad analysis, Tom Cartland had often thought. Especially among those settlers who could barely speak English. There was a passel of them in the hills east of Beaverton, the town closest to Dennison, but southward about twenty-five or twenty-six miles. Dutch, folks called them, but they were actually Swiss and German.

Up here, though, in the lower hills above Dennison there were no foreigners. At least none that Tom Cartland had ever encountered.

But they all tended to take up adjoining claims, and they seemed to always be very closely aligned; if one or two of them came to town for supplies in one of their battered old creaky wagons, there would usually be another three or four neighbours also along. Years back that had been necessary; cowboys and other rangemen such as freighters, mustangers, professional hunters, had harassed the hell out of solitary squatters. They did it to a wagonload of them too, but a lot less. Five or six of those gaunt, sinewy, scar-fisted men could punch a lot of holes in the daylight, and some of those settlers were downright good at that kind of fighting—which rangemen never really excelled in. It made a difference; there had not been an overt assault against settlers in Dennison now in about two years. Not since they'd been coming in groups.

But all that really meant was that rangemen learned to respect bony big fists. It did not mean rangemen were learning to tolerate those people whom they despised and held in monumental contempt.

Tom Cartland had some of that prejudice, inherently and naturally. He had been a rangeman most of his life and even as a lawman he still thought, dressed and acted in the image of a stockman, so when he came quietly down through the soft-hushed night of the upper foothills and ranged along some low little ramparts eyeing rude, sooty orange squares of lamp-glow where the soddies and log shanties stood, he was perfectly willing to believe that someone down there had found that dead man's horse and had confiscated it, saddle, bedroll and all.

To his left, over where a solitary scraped-rawhide window emitted sickly coloured light was where O'Grady and his brood lived. The lad who had found that dead man was O'Grady's eldest, a gangling lad named Michael.

To Cartland's right was the distant pinprick of light coming from the uneven rear log wall of the Brewster cabin, and dead ahead was the nearer and brighter glow of the light from George Cannon's place.

That trapper-trail came down through here, heading arrow-straight for Dennison once it got clear of all the uneven and up-ended back-country.

Cartland settled on the Cannon place, reined down off

the landswell and headed for a post-and-rider fence made of saplings which burly and whiskered George Cannon had erected two-thirds of the full distance of his northernmost boundary.

Cannon was the only one here who really and truly knew what had to be done and worked like a slave to do it. He was also one of the least humble or tractable of the squatters, and he had three large grown sons who were spitting-images of him right down to their willingness to ball up a fist with anyone wearing spurs and carrying a lariat.

Since the last time Cartland had been up through here someone had been working diligently on the boundary-line fence until now it was completely across the rear area which separated George Cannon's holdings from the rougher and forested back-country.

Cartland had to ride in search of a gate. He did not find one but it was hard to imagine anyone building a fence that long and solid without putting a gate somewhere in it.

He got over along the easterly line between Cannon's claim and the westernmost segment of the O'Grady homestead before he could head southward again. Down through here there was a hit-and-miss stretch of indifferent fencing and it was easy to believe O'Grady had done this work down here.

A horse nickered softly out of the darkness and Tom Cartland thought the noise had come from over on the Cannon place but it was hard to tell and the horse did not repeat its amiable little call until he halted to allow his black to look around and locate that invisible animal for him, then it turned out that the call must have come from the O'Grady pasture. His horse swung its head and persisted in staring in that direction.

Tom heard a horse walking forward and swung out of the saddle to get closer so that when the beast hove into view he'd have a good sighting.

It was a big old chestnut work-mare with a flaxen mane and tail. Maybe fifteen, eighteen years back she had been a handsome animal. Now she was old, sway-backed, scarred from work, and peggy when she walked from stiffness in the shoulders. One thing she was not—was a buckskin saddlehorse.

Tom returned to the saddle and headed on southward again. He had not really been very hopeful.

Around him the night remained constant. It was dark and not very well lighted, not even when he got down closer to the Cannon cabin where lamplight shone with a brighter persistence than it usually shone among squatter shacks where people usually had only candlelight. Old Cannon had at least two coal-oil lamps in his house. Among the raffish, dirt-poor settlers of this foothill territory George Cannon must have appeared a man of substance if he dared burn two lamps at once.

Cartland got down where the fence made an abrupt right-angle turn and changed from wood and wire to stark stone where the Cannon menfolk had hauled in rocks from their fields and had started creating a stone fence with them. Tom shook his head. Settlers or not, a man had to respect people who worked that hard, who did not waste

42

even fieldstones, and whose handiwork showed a resolute conviction that here was where they belonged, and here was where nothing would ever be able to shake them loose.

Tom could distantly make out the house so he whistled a little cowtown song—loudly—while walking his black gelding towards the lamp-glow, and true to his expectations a dog with a deep, booming growl rose up somewhere and sounded the alarm in a voice that should have carried at least two miles.

5

AN ACCIDENT

Tom did not see the dog. In fact he never saw him, perhaps because as he came closer to the cabin he did not halt to dismount, not even when he got right up to the tie-rack. That animal was large and unfriendly.

A man came out of the darkness along the east side of the house, said something in a low and guttural tone and the big dog went silent. Then the man distinctly cocked a gun.

Cartland did not have to raise his voice when he announced himself. Once that dog was quiet the night was utterly noiseless.

" It's Cartland from Dennison. Tom Cartland."

Two men softly muttered back and forth then just one of them stepped ahead in the direction of the tie-rack. He was carrying a rifle, not a saddlegun, and it was still cocked when he leaned to peer up through the gloom and to say, " Well, Sheriff—ain't it a mite late at night to be riding around callin' on folks? Climb down if you're a mind to."

Cartland leaned and swung down keeping an eye on Cannon and that big old cocked rifle. When he was on the ground he said, " You're not going to need that thing, George."

44

Cannon shrugged mighty shoulders, then leaned to ease off the hammer and to say, " I expect I won't need it at that, Sheriff; there's three more cocked ones behind me a little ways." He raised his bearded face showing big horsey white teeth in a hard smile. " What can I do for you? You're maybe on your way back from a manhunt and need a place to put up for the night?"

" What I need," stated Tom Cartland, " is some information about a buckskin saddlehorse."

Cannon stood silently for a moment, as though in thought, then leaned down upon his rifle. " Can you describe him, Sheriff?"

Cartland picked up the implication without any trouble. " You got him, have you?"

Cannon hung fire a moment before saying, " Well, we got a buckskin saddlehorse all right, Sheriff. But if you got some notion he's stolen or anything like that you're goin' to have to prove it."

" How long have you had him?" asked Cartland, and George Cannon's silence drew out deeper this time, before he answered.

" Sheriff, you better explain what your interest is, first. Then maybe we can get down to straight talk."

One thing was abundantly clear. The Cannons did not cherish the notion of giving up their buckskin horse. Tom Cartland ducked under the tie-rack, settled his back to it from the nearside facing Cannon, and explained about the dead man, about his interest in a lost horse—and said nothing at all about a moneybelt or six thousand dollars.

45

When he had finished speaking George Cannon turned slightly and said, " You hear that, boys?"

No one answered. No answer was required. Cartland ignored the implication. He had been satisfied Cannon's three stalwart sons would be back there since arriving out front. He made no effort to locate those younger Cannons when he said, " I'd like to hear your story, George."

The bewhiskered older man still leaned upon his upright rifle when he replied, and now he sounded somewhat resigned, or maybe it was more cynical.

" I figured there was something wrong. I bought that horse mid-afternoon today and got him so cheap I figured there had to be something wrong. And, of course, if the lad found the dead feller who likely owned the horse, why that even makes more sense, Sheriff, because I bought him off Will O'Grady, the boy's paw." George Cannon looked disgusted as he hauled upright and stood straight for a change. " Wouldn't you just know it'd have to be something like this?"

Tom said, " You'll get your money back. I'll go over and talk to O'Grady."

" Not the money," growled Cannon. " The horse. We need that horse and he works cattle right well . . . Well, hell, Sheriff; would you like to come inside and drink some coffee with us?"

Tom was sympathetic, so right after declining the coffee he also suggested that this was not the horse the dead man had been riding. He said, " Until I see his outfit, his saddlebags and gatherings, I won't be sure."

Cannon was not particularly interested in that kind of a hope. "We didn't buy the outfit, not even the blankets. O'Grady's still got that stuff as far as I know. We didn't need it and anyway he wanted six dollars for the lot and we didn't have no six dollars left to pay out." Cannon turned. "Will left the outfit over in the shed, Sheriff. Said he'd come over tomorrow in his wagon and take it back with him."

This was more luck than Tom Cartland expected. It may have been more than he deserved. "Mind if I look?" he asked. Cannon turned, called for one of his sons to fetch out a lamp, then led off over in the direction of the rude, long, three-sided shed where the Cannons kept their wagon, their patched old chain-harness, and their own riding equipment, which was in nearly as poor shape as the old set of chain-harness.

But the riding equipment hanging by one stirrup from a lofty wall-peg was good, sound, rangerider's equipment; not new by a long sight, but strong and shiny from use and lightly scarred where ropes and spurs and low tree-limbs had left their marks.

The blanketroll was still tightly wrapped and lashed aft of the cantle. When the lamp finally arrived and the four Cannon menfolk silently watched, Sheriff Cartland took down the bedroll and shook it out. Aside from two moth-eaten old tan army blankets and the groundcloth, there was nothing but a canvas wrapper.

One of the Cannons said, "Huh; where did he carry his razor? Look in the saddle-pockets, Mister Cartland."

47

Tom had misgivings. It had not surprised him that the Cannons had not been curious enough to ransack the bedroll and saddlebags, but clearly someone had, and it was a reasonable guess that the ransacker had been Will O'Grady, who was by nature that kind of individual.

The saddlebags were empty.

George Cannon grunted and when the lawman stood up to dust off his knees the elder Cannon had a dry comment to make. " All Will told us was that he'd tracked down this stray buckskin and it was fully rigged out, and he figured it must have been on the trail for a lot of days judging from the looks and all, so I figured—well—I just figured there wouldn't be anyone lookin' for the horse if he come a long distance."

Tom had nothing to say about this statement. " Where's the horse?" he asked, and followed as the Cannons turned, the stalwart youth with the lamp upraised walking ahead.

Most squatters had corrals but not very many of them had the strongly set up kind that the Cannons possessed. The buckskin horse was drowsing in the pleasant night near a hand-made log feeder which still held a few wisps of timothy hay.

Tom leaned and studied the horse. He was thick-chested, powerfully muscled, had a nice set of good eyes in a small, broad head, and was not just short-backed but was also powerfully butted. He showed indications of having been ridden long and hard; even for a buckskin, he showed a lot of recent rough usage.

George Cannon came up and leaned beside the lawman.

He said, " Jess, hold the light a mite closer," and when this had been done the older man thrust forth a ham-sized hand to point. " Sheriff, you'll be interested in the brand. There it is; left shoulder, the letters J L K." Cannon turned. " You see 'em?"

They were easy to see. Like all buckskins this one had a black skin under the tan hair. Where there was no hair because of scar tissue the brand showed up very well, and this too was something Tom Cartland had wanted to see.

He straightened back. " I'll tell you what I'd like to do, George, if it's all right with you. I'd like to leave the horse here, and the outfit, until I've run down that brand, and until I've found the stuff O'Grady took out of the saddle-bags and bedroll. This may not be the horse which belonged to that dead feller. I got no way of knowing until I've done a lot more rummagin' around."

Cannon was combing his full beard with bent fingers and gazing in at the horse with the look of a man who liked good animals. Without turning he said, " It's all right with me, and I hope you don't find out nothing that'll make you come after him."

Tom turned back towards the horse. " How much did you give O'Grady?"

" Two dollars and half pound of chewing tobacco I brought back from Beaverton last autumn." After a long pause, and perhaps because he had traded for the buckskin for so little that his conscience was troubling him, George Cannon also said, " Well, Sheriff, to a feller like you who makes maybe twelve, fifteen dollars a month, two dollars

49

ain't much. But me and my lads got to cut and swathe and load and haul in an awful lot of wild hay and peddle it around town, to make us two dollars."

Without any warning Cartland's black horse around front at the tie-rack suddenly sat back, snapped the tie-shank, whirled with a wild snorting whistle and broke away in a high-headed lunging run.

Two of the young Cannons rushed around there, one of them cursing with the monumental sensation of purest disgust any horseman would have felt over such an incident, but regardless of their haste and their language, they did not even get out there in time to catch a sight of the black horse.

All that remained was the frayed end of the tie-rope draped disconsolately from the cross-member at the hitch-rack.

By the time the others got around there the father of those stalwart young men had guessed more than the others, had veered over alongside the house to feel along a length of old rusty chain until he had a broken link in his fingers, then he said, " The wolf got loose."

Cartland scowled. " That dog . . .?"

" He ain't a dog, Sheriff, he's a wolf, but he's about the best pet we've ever had. Just got one bad habit . . ."

Tom swore softly, " Gawddammit—just one bad habit—rushing out and scaring the whey out of tethered horses."

George Cannon was embarrassed and chagrined. " I don't rightly know what to say, Mister Cartland. I thought the chain—well—we never let him run loose at night and

I figured this here piece of chain would hold him easy. Except that he's been growing so much this past year."

The stalwart young man named Jess offered a solution. " I'd be right proud to ride down and hunt up your horse, Sheriff, and you can go inside and set with paw and drink coffee until I get back ... And don't worry, I'll get him. I got a knack for it even in the dark."

Tom did not dispute Jess's ability to track a noisily running horse in the darkness, but he would have disputed Jess's ability to catch his black horse because that black could outrun anything around, and he'd already got about a two-mile head-start. Plus the fact that Tom Cartland had seen the horses the Cannons rode; they were just a smidgin better than most squatter-horses which meant Jess would never even get close to the black until he got down to Dennison, which would be where the black would rush to.

He thanked Jess, simply said, " He'll head for home. No sense in you riding all night," and turned towards Jess's father. " I'd like to borrow a critter to get back to town on. I'll fetch him back tomorrow when I ride back over this way to see Will O'Grady."

The elder Cannon nodded without any hesitation. " If you want, Sheriff, you're plumb welcome to ride the new buckskin. He's the best saddle animal we got. Otherwise, we got some combination horses which are pretty big and clumsy."

Cartland had seen those combination riding and pulling horses. If he ever appeared down the rain roadway of Dennison astride such a beast, even at night ... " I'll bring the buckskin back tomorrow," he said. " And now I'll have to borrow that saddle from the shed too, George." He paused to listen. They all did, but there was no longer even an echo of shod hooves southward.

One of the big young men softly said, " That dang wolf. I'll tan his britches for him. I've larruped him fifty times for runnin' at horses like that. Thing is, Sheriff, he don't know he's not a dog, you see; he don't know that the smell of a wolf to most saddle horses is enough to make him dang near have a heart seizure."

Tom Cartland's frame of mind could have agreed with the part about larruping some hide off the wolf, and as for the rest of it, he did not care a tinker's damn. He just wanted to get back to town ahead of daylight—if he could.

But if he'd come right down to it, this hadn't been a very auspicious day for him right from the time he arose this morning and could not find his razor when he went out back behind the rooming-house to the wash-rack to make himself presentable.

And now this.

George Cannon sent one of his sons for the buckskin horse, then walked disconsolately beside Sheriff Cartland over to the shed where the saddle was.

Finally, Cartland began to feel sorry for the burly older man. Cannon was so humiliated he fairly oozed embarrassment. Tom tried to be charitable by saying, " It could have happened in town, too, I expect. Not with a darned wolf, but there's big dogs in town who run at horses."

" It's our fault," Cannon replied. " We been puttin' off

tradin' for a new chain at Mister Markham's store because we just never trade for nothing we don't downright need real bad, you see. And the blessed wolf's been on that tether almost two years and he don't weigh like a pup any longer. He's just plain got too big and stout and we knew it. We just didn't do anything about it." Cannon looked steadily at Cartland. " I'd feel a lot better if you'd come inside and drink a cup of coffee with me, Sheriff. Sure don't look right, you bein' set afoot by our carelessness then not even being invited inside."

" Well, maybe after I've saddled up . . ."

" The boys'll look after that for you. The least they can do, Sheriff. Come along; I've got a bottle of fresh squeezings right from our still up in the mountains to put some muscle into the coffee with. Come along, Sheriff . . ."

Tom went.

6

A CLUE

Cannon's remark about the whisky being fresh from the still had to be correct because it was as transparent as water when he splashed a little into each of the chipped crockery cups which he had previously poured coffee into.

He was a widower, which Tom Cartland knew because he remembered when Elisabeth Cannon was taken off during an early springtime epidemic of lung fever. His three sons had of late been hiring out now and then to the big cattle interests. It was said down around Dennison that they were turning into passable rangemen.

As Tom eased tiredly down at the oilcloth-covered table near the wood-stove and watched his bearded big thick host between stove and table, he glanced around the cabin's interior with interest. He had not only never been inside the Cannon residence before, he had only rarely been in any squatter houses.

When George sat down with a sigh and leaned on the table he said, " We was settin' around takin' turns readin' aloud from The Book." He nodded towards a large limp old Bible with the initials E.C. embossed on the red leather cover.

Tom understood. Most families did that. Not every night, but fairly often, and usually for as long as their children were small. For settlers living this far from town it was a substitute for Sunday church-going, among other things.

" Then the wolf set up a hollering and we figured it had to be a two-legged varmint from the kind of bark he was making." George lifted the cup and sipped, set it down and shook his head. " I'm sure put out for the way he scairt off your horse, Sheriff."

As far as Tom Cartland was concerned that was water under the bridge. He glanced around looking for a clock. There was none. These people rarely had what they considered luxuries and what townsfolk considered necessities.

Cannon saw the look though and shrugged as he said, " It'll be a little better'n maybe ten, eleven o'clock, Sheriff." He crookedly smiled. " An hour one way or the other don't much matter . . . About the buckskin horse . . . even if it turns out he ain't the animal that dead feller was riding, how would the law look on him being a stray and all?"

" They got a newspaper down at Beaverton," Cartland explained. " The law says he's got to be advertised three days straight running, and after that if no one comes along to prove ownership and to claim him, you can put in a claim for feed and care and take him."

Cannon combed his beard gravely. " It's been a long while since we've owned any good-using animals, Sheriff. Not since we left Missouri to come out here, take up a claim and put down new roots. It's been a hard half-dozen years, for a fact, but we're gainin', a little at a time. Got thirty head of cows, now, finally, and got three old bad-off horses—and the buckskin—but we're stubborn folk and we're going to keep at it, back-breakin' or not."

The older man continued to gravely comb his beard and sit there gazing steadily over at the rangeman-sheriff.

"Folks got a right to think of us as they do. If someone come along and took over land I'd been usin' free for thirty years I wouldn't take kindly to it, either. But you see—we couldn't get back to Missouri if we hitched up and tried. No money left, teams are worn out."

Tom Cartland shifted a trifle uneasily on his chair. He had never liked being taken into a person's confidence. He did not like it now so he attempted to switch the topic of conversation by saying, "You people put up mighty fine hay. Folks down around Dennison got so's they depend on it. I guess you created a market, and that's a start."

One of the big younger Cannons came to the doorway to say the horse was rigged out and tethered at the rack out front. Then he also said, "The wolf come back, paw. Want me to whale hell out of him?"

George Cannon stopped combing his beard, shot Tom Cartland a look, noisily cleared his throat, then said, "Well now, son, you know he's just a dumb animal. He didn't mean to do wrong . . . but see if you can't maybe double up the chain so's he can't bust loose again." Cannon then busily emptied his cup as though signifying the visit was finished, then leaned to arise without glancing over at the lawman.

At the door while still avoiding Tom's glance, George

Cannon gallantly stepped back for the lawman to walk out first, and as he closed the door after himself he sniffed and said, " There's a light chill settin' in."

There was indeed a chill to the late night air, and by dawn it would be colder still, but as Sheriff Cartland swung up across leather he was not particularly aware of it. That popskull-whisky in the black coffee would prevent him from feeling cold for several hours yet.

He reiterated his intention of returning from town the next day, thanked the Cannons for their co-operation and hospitality, and turned the buckskin horse. The animal answered his slightest touch of the reins. He looked back and Jess, one of the younger Cannons, said, " Mighty well-broke horse, Sheriff. You'll see."

It was indeed a fact that whoever had broken the buckskin to saddle and to rein had been a very accomplished horseman. Several hours later when Tom had the few scattered town-lights in sight down across the velvety darkness, he and the buckskin had got fairly well acquainted. When he reached the upper roadway leading down through town he decided it was a shame for settlers to own a horse as good as this one, and rode through to the south end of Dennison to swing out of the saddle and whistle up the liverybarn nighthawk—who had been sound asleep in the harness room.

The man did not open his mouth. He stalked forth, took the reins from Tom Cartland without even a nod, turned and shuffled down the runway leading the buckskin away. There always had to be some confounded idiot who didn't know enough to go to bed at a decent hour like decent folk, come along and roust a man from his horse-blanket in the harness-room! Never failed!

Cartland did not go directly to his room at the boarding-house. He went first to the jailhouse office and out back into the storeroom to haul three musty looseleaf binders back to the front room and put them atop his desk while he turned up the lamp and got comfortable in the desk-chair.

It took him more than an hour to find it, and he first ploughed through the registered brands of Colorado and Nevada before turning the pages of the Arizona brandbook and coming up with the entry ' J L K 1/s—Kildare, Jethro K—Kildare's Indian Wells Ranch, Casa Verde, Arizona '.

' J L K 1/s ' signified that the J L K brand was put on the 1/s, left shoulder.

Tom yawned, looked over where the cold iron stove stood with the equally as cold granite ware coffeepot atop it, decided against going through all the work it would be necessary to go through to fire up some coffee, and settled down to writing a letter to the Town Council, Casa Verde, Arizona. He described the buckskin horse, the dead man he thought might have been riding the buckskin, asking about the man's identity and record around Casa Verde, and ended up suggesting that the rider may have been a wanted fugitive. But he did not mention the moneybelt nor the money.

He licked the envelope, plugged on a postage stamp,

blew down the lamp-mantle to plunge his office into darkness and left the building on his way over to the slot in the front wall of the general store where the postal office occupied a tiny cubicle, and after having shoved the Arizona letter into the slot he finally headed for the rooming-house.

He was tired, but he also felt slightly elated. This morning, which had started out badly, he had not felt that this would be one of his better days. When his horse ran off up in the foothills he had felt more convinced than ever this was one of his bad days. But now, after having made at least some headway, and having sent off the letter which he felt certain would start an enlightening chain reaction for him, he changed his mind and decided that actually, this was a *good* day.

If he had not been so tired and in such haste to get to his room it probably would have occurred to him that this was not the same day at all, that the bad day had ended somewhere between the Cannon homestead and town when the time had passed beyond midnight to the first hour of a brand new day.

The following morning someone banging on the door of his room brought him wide awake. He yelled out for them to slack off or they'd wake the whole darned town, and the garrulous, unmistakable voice of Brutus Tolbert came right back saying, "Ain't no decent folks still abed, for heaven's sake. It's past eight o'clock. You figurin' on sleeping the clock around, do you? ... I got your black gelding down at the barn. Come in sometime last night, saddled and bridled. He's stepped on your reins and broke them off up close to the bit."

Cartland yawned, felt his beard-stubbled face, spun half around to come upright in a sitting position upon the edge of the bed, and said, "I'll be down to get him directly. Thanks for letting me know."

The show of gratitude must have encouraged Brutus. He called through the door again. "And I see you found that buckskin you was lookin' for."

Cartland looked balefully at the door. "I'll see you later," he growled, and this time Tolbert took the cue and went loping down the stairs.

It usually took close to an hour to get cleaned up and ready for the new day when a man lived alone at the boarding-house. The longest delay was waiting for other men to vacate the wash-rack out back. This morning there was no one ahead of Cartland so he got to shave and scrub and get ready without any delay. But there was also a penalty; they did not serve breakfast at the boarding-house but once, and if boarders missed out for whatever reason, they either had to head for the cafe down alongside the harness shop, or go without.

Tom Cartland went down to the cafe. Here, too, because it was almost ten o'clock when he walked in, there was no wait. But he got a sidelong look from the cafeman, an old rangerider who had half-frozen his feet one time and could no longer ride much nor work inside a corral on the ground. He said, "Wish I had a lawman's job and could eat breakfast in the middle of the day."

Cartland sighed to himself, said nothing, and when the food finally arrived and the walrus-moustached cafeman leaned down to make another remark, Sheriff Cartland aimed a fork at the cafeman's gullet and quietly said, "Now Arnold, you better watch yourself or I'll hustle you out back and stamp hell out of your toes."

The cafeman clumped over behind his drapery with the improbably enormous cabbage-roses on it where he did his cooking, and said, "I wasn't goin' to say nothing about *that*. I was just goin' to tell you that Doc Bannon was around here last night lookin' for you . . . Sheriff, for a fact the older you get the worse your disposition is getting!"

Tom paused in his eating to reflect that there simply was no way in this life to come out ahead about two-thirds of the time, then hunched over and went back to his meal.

He did not go in search of Doctor Bannon until after he had walked down, got his black horse, and had led it up the west-side alley to his shed out behind the jailhouse to care for it. Because of that, by the time he got up to Joshua Bannon's cottage the doctor was gone. So was his harness-horse and his fringed-top buggy, and that meant of course Doctor Bannon had been called to make a visit beyond town.

Back at the jailhouse office firing up the wood-stove to make a fresh pot of coffee, Cartland was visited by waspish old Amos Jennings from over at the general store. Amos handed Cartland some mail and said, "Most folks pick up their post, Sheriff, and don't expect other folks to deliver it to them," then turned with a loud snort and departed.

Cartland pitched the mail atop his desk and continued working with the stove.

A dogfight erupted up in front of the gun shop, some loud profanity accompanied all the other racket, and by the time Sheriff Cartland got over to the door of his office to lean and look up in that direction, the dogs had been parted by the gunsmith, who had nearly drowned them with a big bucket of flung water, but the owners of those fighting dogs were now growling, facing one another and stiffly backing and filling.

Cartland yelled out. "You fellers break that up before I come up there and crack your darned heads for you. *I mean it.*"

The gunsmith, still holding his wooden bucket and attired in his oily old apron, said something to the stiff-standing dog-owners, and the two men turned and walked away from one another.

Doctor Bannon's topbuggy came whipping southward ahead of a high dust-banner, entered town and scarcely slackened pace as Doc drive right on down to the livery barn and halted, climbed out with his black satchel, and stood a moment beating dust from his clothing with his hat, which when he had finished, was hopelessly out of shape, but Doc crushed it down over his grey thatch and went stalking up in the direction of the jailhouse where he no doubt had seen Tom Cartland standing in his office doorway as unmindful of his personal appearance as he usually was.

Tom left the door open and went back to his stove to adjust the damper, peer in at the fire to make certain it was burning properly, then he set two cups on the desk instead of just one cup and when Doctor Bannon stumped in looking around, Cartland pointed to a chair and said, " The coffee'll be maybe ten minutes. Where you been so early?"

Bannon blinked. " Early? It's noon or better and I didn't leave town until eight." He went to the chair, sank down with the satchel on his lap, with the battered hat atop his head, and gazed thoughtfully at Sheriff Cartland. " I just had a hunch. In fact I woke up this morning with this feeling—so I got the rig and headed for the Hartman horse camp and there she was, springy as a young heifer."

" Who was springy?"

" That Messican girl who cooks for the Hartman riding crew. Name is Letriana. Isn't that a pretty name?"

" Yeah. She had a baby?"

" By gawd, Tom, right while I was there. Now you can't call for any better timing than that can you?"

" I didn't know she was married, Doc."

" She isn't. But sonny, you don't have to be married to have a baby." Doc leaned, set the satchel on the floor beside his chair and went to groping through his pockets until he found what he'd been searching for.

Tom Cartland almost groaned aloud as Joshua Bannon held up one of his evil small cigars, smiled benignly at it and dug around until he'd found a match to light it with.

63

The roadside door was still open, for which Sheriff Cart-land was grateful.

When he was thoroughly comfortable again, Doctor Bannon said, " I think I convinced her to name the baby Tom."

Sheriff Cartland slowly stiffened as he stared across at the older man. " That's not very funny," he said. " You damned well know how folks gossip even when they don't have anything to base their talk on."

Doc blew smoke. " I didn't have you in mind. She told me the daddy was that Massican cowboy named Tom Velarde who's been wrangling horses for the Hartmans for . . . I'll be damned; have you been seein' that girl? How's come you to jump to such a conclusion, Sheriff, unless you got a guilty conscience?"

" I don't have a guilty conscience," exploded Tom Cart-land, getting slightly red in the face. " I just met the girl once, last autumn when I had to take some legal papers out to Mister Hartman. I didn't even know her name. And while I'm glad she had a son and didn't run into any trouble calving, this darned conversation is getting . . ."

" All right. All right, Sheriff. Nothing to get mad over."

" Why were you looking for me last night?" yelled Tom Cartland, " And who is mad, gawddammit!"

Doctor Bannon eyed the younger man, chewed on his little cigar, and finally said softly, " I just wanted to tell you I described that ivory-handled sixgun to old Merritt the gunsmith at the saloon last night and he said if he could see it, could take the grips off, there might be a name and a date inside, that very often gunsmiths who turn out those special sixguns do that—put their names inside on the handles."

7

THE O'GRADY VISIT

Tom Cartland told Doctor Bannon of his adventures the previous night up along the foothill-country, and when he had finished Joshua Bannon was sitting in thought and forgetting to puff on the Mex stogie, so of course it went out.

" I've been through Casa Verde several times," stated Doctor Bannon. " It's not much. Larger than Dennison but that's not necessarily saying very much for it as a town. It's down along the Gila not too far from the border. One of those towns that wouldn't last six months if there wasn't an army post nearby. But of course I don't know anyone down there, least of all anyone named Kildare." Doc considered his cold cigar but did not relight it as he shoved it back between strong, worn teeth.

" You've darned well made a start, Sheriff," he murmured, leaning to retrieve the small black satchel and to stand up. " What's the buckskin horse worth?"

Cartland misinterpreted Bannon's thought and dryly said, " He's worth a hell of a lot more than you got coming for laying that feller out," and also arose, stepped around from behind the desk to go to the door with Doctor

Bannon.

The older man looked pained. " I wasn't thinking of what I have coming, confound it."

" Well, I'd guess the buckskin is worth maybe as much as thirty-five dollars."

Doctor Bannon halted in his tracks. " That much?"

" He's one hell of a saddle horse, Doc. Reins better'n most horses I've sat on and doesn't seem to have a single bad habit. He packed me down from the foothills in record time and is easy to ride. In fact, I'm going to ride him back up there to the Cannon place this afternoon, lead my black, and leave him up there for the Cannons to look after until it's settled about him one way or another. Like I told you, they bought him off Will O'Grady."

Doc sighed. " Naturally. The lad got home, told his paw about finding the dead man under the juniper tree, and Will went out immediately and hunted down the horse."

Tom was of the same opinion but all he said now was, " Time will tell."

Doc cocked an eye upwards. " You won't get back until after dark again. Why not wait until morning to take him up there?"

" Because I told Cannon I'd fetch him back today."

Bannon stood a moment longer out front of the jailhouse building looking critically back at the younger man, then he wagged his head and without another word went hiking up in the direction of his cottage.

There actually was more than just the matter of having told George Cannon he would return the buckskin today, which motivated Sheriff Cartland to go round back to rig out his black horse, then go down to rig out the buckskin and to afterwards head up the alleyway out of town. He particularly wanted to talk to William O'Grady; wanted to see everything O'Grady had removed from the blanketroll and saddlebags of the buckskin horse's saddle.

What he had guessed so far—that the buckskin horse came from the ranch of a man named Kildare over in Ariozona—did not tie the dead man to the buckskin, and this was what Sheriff Cartland needed right now more than he needed anything else which might have to do with that horse—or with that dead man. If there were such evidence, it would be among the personal effects O'Grady had gleaned before he had peddled the horse to George Cannon.

He had left Dennison a little earlier today than he had left it yesterday. In fact he had ridden forth from town only shortly after high noon, while yesterday—for an excellent reason—he had waited until the afternoon was well advanced towards sundown before riding out.

It was a bell-clear, magnificent springtime day. Two months from now there would be shimmery heatwaves this time of day, and the frail wild grass would be curing in the stem, but right now the air was fragrant with pine-scent from the far-away hills, and there were tiny little, perfectly detailed, wildflowers almost anywhere a rider chose to look.

Tom Cartland talked to the two horses. Most rangemen did that and after enough time had passed a horse got so that he could understand intonations, inflexions, general nuances of human articulation. Today, Cartland's black and the husky little buckskin walked right along perfectly satisfied from the sound of that voice that the man up there was in a fine and mellow mood.

Which he was.

The only time his mood underwent even a slight change was when he got up within sight of the O'Grady claim, and saw the slightly undersized man out in the yard in front of his poorly-built log barn removing harness from an old team of seal-brown horses.

He knew Will O'Grady about as well as he knew any of the foothill people, and while he had reservations about all of them, he had the most reservations about O'Grady, who was a wiry, narrow-faced man with sly pale eyes and an elfin look about him which always put Sheriff Cartland in mind of someone whose craftiness never rested.

Still, when he rode up and drew rein and saw the way O'Grady was eyeing the buckskin horse, he let none of his wariness show as he said, " Fine afternoon, beautiful weather. It's beginning to look like we'll have a good grass year."

The sly-faced older man turned to drape old harness over a rear wagon-wheel and to turn back with a forced smile. " For a fact it'll be a good grass year," O'Grady responded. " There's already feed throughout the foothill's better'n anything before since I come out here, Sheriff . . . And you'll want to know about that horse. I just come back from Cannon's place so I knew you had him—and the outfit." O'Grady did not take his eyes off the buckskin to look up at the mounted lawman. " As you know m'lad

Michael found the dead feller down close to town a short while back, and went at once an' told you, like the good lad he is."

Tom waited to be invited to dismount, which was simple range courtesy. O'Grady kept looking at the buckskin horse and talking, and never did extend that invitation.

" You'll understand how hard it is with us folks up along the foothill-country, Sheriff, and how we need every little boon the Good Lord sends us, so you'll understand as soon as Michael come home and told me about the dead man, and all, why naturally I figured it out that feller'd had a horse and I went right out to hunt him down."

Cartland leaned, swung from the saddle and stood beside his horse. " Where did you find him? he asked. " I mean—how far from town and on what part of the range?"

O'Grady made a vague arm-wave as he replied. " West, Sheriff, and east a ways. I thought I'd go down to them twin trees and pick up the sign and track him from there, but instead I sort of sashayed over west a few miles, and cut some recent sign out there and went after it." O'Grady finally raised his pale eyes. " It was the buckskin horse. But I'm not convinced he belonged to that dead feller at all."

Tom thought back to the story O'Grady had told George Cannon, decided that O'Grady had to now also try and convince the lawman he was innocent of any possible wrongdoing, and decided to head off some big windy cock-and-bull story before it got under way, so he said, " Where are the things you took out of the saddlebags and the bedroll?"

70

Will O'Grady turned, looked at his patient-standing team, then moved up to unhook them at the collar and lead them off the tongue as he answered the sheriff.

"Got it all in the barn, in a box in there, Sheriff, but I figured to fetch it on down to Dennison next time I was down that way, and turn it over to the law."

Tom said, "Sure you did," under his breath, stepped up to tie his black horse to a ring in the side of the barn, and took the buckskin horse over to a corral-stringer to also tether him, then he followed O'Grady into the log barn where it was as dark as though evening were already over the land.

The box O'Grady brought over held some sacks of smoking tobacco, a carton of bullets for a .45 Colt, a complete change of underclothes right down to the socks, and even a clean spare neckerchief—used instead as a handkerchief by most rangemen—and a letter folded into a worn, limp envelope from which the name on the front had been completely obliterated from continual abrasive rubbing against other things in a saddlebag. But the contents of the letter were clearly readable. They had been written in a round, wide-spaced variety of penmanship someone had learned in school, and the name at the bottom of the letter was 'Anne.'

That was all, just the name 'Anne' without a surname or an address.

The letter started out by simply saying 'I never thought I could miss anyone as much as I have missed you this past six months.'

It did not mention the recipient by his name, and it did not mention other people, places, even days or seasons. it simply went on for the full page talking of 'Anne's' anguished love over the loss of the person to whom she had written the letter, and when Sheriff Cartland finished reading it and glanced up, he could tell by Will O'Grady's expression that the settler had also read the letter.

O'Grady said, "It don't help none, does it?"

Cartland folded the letter, pocketed the thin-worn envelope and leaned without speaking to rummage further in the box, and to eventually straighten up shooting a look towards Will O'Grady.

"You're sure there was nothing else?" he asked, and saw a flicker cross O'Grady's eyes so he stood up to his full height and fixed the older, shorter man with an expression of unmistakable doubt.

O'Grady fished in a pocket, brought forth a heavy gold watch with an engraved hunting scene on the case. The watch also had one of those ornate very heavy gold chains with it. Looking almost sick, O'Grady passed those things over without looking up and without saying a word.

Cartland studied the watch, which was gold and clearly hand-assembled and engraved, and worth a lot of money. Then he popped open the front cover and saw the initials J L K engraved there in the midst of some very elegant and flowery curlicues. A watchmaker's name in Chicago was clearly printed inside the case in the back.

O'Grady said, "It don't run, Sheriff. Just a busted timepiece."

Cartland snapped the case closed, pocketed the watch and eyed O'Grady. The man was not at all above plundering a dead man, and a lost horse, and yet he had actually not broken a law. He had undoubtedly intended to keep and sell the horse, the saddle and bridle, and probably even the gold watch, but except for the horse he had not really sold any of it—yet—and now the horse was reclaimed.

There was nothing Tom Cartland could use as a basis for taking O'Grady back to Dennison and locking him up, although he had a strong hankering to do it anyway.

In the end he took the box of private effects out to his own saddle and filled the bags out there, then flung aside the box and when O'Grady came over looking decidedly unhappy, Tom said, "You darned well knew enough to fetch that horse to town for impounding when you found him, and don't go and tell me some darned lie about it." He untied his horse, led it over to also untie the buckskin horse, then as he turned to face O'Grady again, he said, "I think you'd better give the Cannon's back their two dollars for the buckskin. If it turns out later he's up for grabs, that'll be a different story."

Cartland mounted the black gelding, draped the tag-end of his lead-shank around the horn and sat a moment longer looking down. There wasn't much else to say to O'Grady, and even if there had been, it would have been a waste of time to say it, so Cartland turned and rode back out of the yard, but this time heading westerly over towards the Cannon claim.

As soon as he was out of the yard and had put Will

O'Grady out of his mind, he turned back to developing the thought which had occurred to him when he had flipped open that watch-case and had seen those three initials in there.

It could very easily have been a simple matter of horse-theft for that dead man to have been riding that J L K buckskin gelding. Horse-thieves were a dime a dozen over in Arizona, exactly as they were in New Mexico.

But it was pushing coincidental possibilities beyond the realm of probability to assume that the same man who stole a J L K horse and also managed to steal Jethro L. Kildare's gold pocketwatch.

It was far more probable, now, that Jethro L. Kildare had been caught out, perhaps between his cow-outfit and some town such as Casa Verde, by an outlaw who had taken Kildare's horse, his gold pocket-watch, and just possibly that six thousand dollars in the moneybelt as well. It was an awful lot of money for a cowman to be riding around with, but there were many explanations, such as Kildare having just sold a big bunch of cattle and was heading home after having been paid for them, but whatever the reason, Tom Cartland was beginning to believe more and more that the man he and Doc Bannon had planted was a horse-thief, a highwayman, and also a murderer.

8

THE CANNON'S

George Cannon was over at the forge in his shoeing-shed when Sheriff Cartland entered the yard. The wolf was not on his chain, something Tom looked for before riding towards the shed with the smoke billowing out its smokestack.

If any of the other Cannons were around the lawman did not see them, and as soon as the elder Cannon looked out and saw who was crossing towards him from the direction of the house, he put aside his tools, gave the bellows an extra downwards sweep to make sure the coals did not die while he was talking out front, and patted the old brown horse he had been shoeing on the rump as he stepped past and tugged off the muleskin shoeing apron.

" Afternoon to you," he said amiably, pitching the apron aside. " You talk to O'Grady yet?"

Tom nodded. " He said he'd been over here."

Cannon gestured. " Get down, Sheriff. Let me take them horses and look after them for you, then we can sit in the shade for a spell."

Cartland glanced around. " You alone?"

" Yes. Our cows drifted towards Hartman's horse range

so the boys went off to turn them back. Never had trouble with old Hartman, and from what I've heard about how he acts when he's been fired up, I don't want any trouble with him."

Cannon tied the black in the shade, looked a little scepti- cally at the condition of his feet, then took the buckskin over and turned him back into the same pole corral he had come out of last night.

As he turned back he said, " Sheriff, that black of yours sure needs a reset," and Cartland agreed without even looking at his horse.

" His feet grow faster'n any horse I've ever owned. I've yet to wear out a set of shoes on him before they have to be reset."

Cannon reached for an old rag to mop his face and neck with as he said, " If you got an hour or so I'd be plumb willing to reset them shoes. Cost you a half dollar less'n they'll do it in Dennison."

Tom was willing, but he had never seen any of Cannon's shoeing so he turned to study the feet of that big old drowsing bay nearby. He had only been shod in front and trimmed behind. It was a professional job.

Tom went to a horseshoe keg which had been turned upside down as a chair, sat down and said, " He's all yours, George." Then, as the burly man led the bay away and brought over the black, tied both stirrups across the saddle- seat so they would not hit him in the head and face while he was working, Cartland told him of his visit at the O'Grady place.

Cannon finished preparing the black horse, and pumped his forge a few times before tieing the apron back around and spitting on his hands as he advanced upon the black horse, his mind only half on what the lawman had been saying. As he picked up a forefoot he said, " He got any bad habits, Sheriff, like halter-pulling or biting my rear when I'm bending over his foot?"

" No bad habits of any kind," stated Cartland. " If they come to me with bad habits I trade them off the very next day." As Cannon went to work with the pullers Tom said, " Did O'Grady happen to mention any of the things he found in the bedroll and saddlebags of the buckskin horse?"

Cannon was paring with sure, long strokes of his curled farrier's knife when he answered. " Not a thing. Until this morning when he come over, and you'd already been here and I told him that, he didn't even act like there was anything on the saddle." Cannon reached for his nippers and went to work on the lengthy rim of the overgrown hoof, which, fortunately was soft—as they all were this time of year when the earth was still moist. " Thing is, Sheriff, a man hadn't ought to talk about his neighbours. Now then, I'm not bein' mean when I say you just cannot believe what Will O'Grady tells you. I don't know how well you are acquainted with him, but we've lived next to him for several years and we *do* know him. He just plain lies a lot, I'm sorry to say."

Tom glanced down. Bewhiskered George Cannon had acted pained throughout his statement regarding O'Grady. Tom could understand how he felt and could sympathise with him. On the other hand Cannon had not told him a blessed thing he either had not already known or had not suspected.

A horseman entering the yard caught Cartland's attention. He arose, went to the front of the shed and leaned to look out. It was that younger Cannon named Jess, and the horse he was astride looked pretty well ridden down. From back in the shed Cannon said, " Who is it?"

" One of your boys; the one you called Jess last night."

Cannon straightened up with his tools in hand and came over to also look. " Now what's he doin' back here, they couldn't have got the cattle turned this soon—I don't think." Cannon raised his voice. " Jess! Over here at the shoeing-shed!"

The tall, wide-shouldered young man swung to earth and walked over leading his tired horse. He nodded briefly at the sheriff then faced his father.

" They been spooked," he reported. " In the night we figured, but anyway somethin' scairt 'em and now they won't drive, they just want to split off and run." The stalwart youth looked at the horse behind him. " We don't have nothing that'll turn 'em, paw. We need one feller to head 'em, and the rest of us could then take over and keep 'em pointed in this direction."

An idea crossed Sheriff Cartland's mind. " Suppose I took the buckskin horse," he said, " and went back out there with you. My black'd turn 'em, but your paw's resetting his shoes so I'll ride the buckskin. That'd make four of us— one on stockhorse. What d'you think?"

Jess nodded while looking at his father. " It'd work," he said. " Paw . . . ?"

" Sure enough," replied the elder Cannon. " Sheriff, we'd sure be obliged to you."

Tom went after the buckskin and while he was across the yard George asked his son how far out their panicky cattle were, and instead of a direct answer Jess said, " Not very far, paw, but that ain't it. The way they run when we first come into sight made it clear whoever spooked them was men on horseback. Wasn't wolves or bears or lions, it was men on horseback."

Old Cannon scowled. " Hartman?"

Jess did not know. " Maybe, maybe not. We didn't see a soul and we sashayed around a little lookin' for them— whoever they was. But maybe they spooked the herd last night." Jess looked around. " The sheriff got anythin' special on his mind?"

" Not that he's let on," answered Jess's father, and reverted to the topic most interesting to him at this moment. " You fellers do what he says. He's an experienced rangeman, by his looks."

They stopped speaking as Cartland returned across the yard and tied the tractable buckskin then went into the shed to strip his black and haul the rigging out to the fresher horse.

It did not take long to get saddled. As Tom turned his buckskin then mounted, he said, " If they aren't out too far this hadn't ought to take long, George," then he led off out of the yard with Jess pointing the direction they had to

79

travel.

The elder Cannon leaned in his shed doorway gazing after them for a while before turning back to work on the black horse.

The day was warm and beautiful. It was mantled here and there with lean shadows which had just begun to appear on the lee side of the few tall-standing pine trees which had been allowed to survive the log-hunter's axe when the Cannons had first settled their claim.

Jess pointed out landmarks but as a matter of fact Tom Cartland knew this area as well as anyone, he'd been hunting it for years. When Jess finally drew down to a walk and raised a hand, Cartland beat him to the announcement.

" That's the boundary line between you folks and Hartman's horse range, down where those witness-trees are standing in a little clump. And the line cuts straight across and goes up the mountainside north of here a couple miles."

Jess lowered his hand to the saddlehorn. " You know your bailiwick," he said, and jutted his jaw. " Yonder's some of the darned critters."

The cattle Tom saw were high-headed and acted as wary as wild animals. They were over across a dip and a rise, were poised for flight atop a low, wide landswell. Tom shook his head. " Whatever scairt them sure did a hell of a good job of it. Let's split up. Go far out and around on each side and see can we get behind them."

Someone sang out from a considerable distance. Tom did not see him but Jess did. " My brothers," he announced. " Off north-west."

"Don't let them get in behind those critters until I've laid a scent up the north-easterly range," stated Tom, and reined the buckskin away to begin his wide and deep roundabout half-circle.

The cattle watched intently but as long as none of the mounted men came any closer than they now were, the cattle did not seem willing to run.

It was impossible to count heads from Tom's position, about a mile eastward, but he guessed there had to be about fifteen or twenty heads of cattle up yonder, as he eased ahead and loped the buckskin on its way. If the Cannons had another fifteen or twenty head, they would probably be able to find them and get them heading for home once the scent of this initial gather was laid down in the right direction. Cattle would follow the scent of other cattle with absolute trust.

Tom achieved the position he sought, eventually, while the sun began reddening a little as it made an overhead low sweep towards the westernmost peaks and ridges. When he thought it would be proper to close in, he stood in the stirrups, saw three distant riders, flagged towards them with his hat, then eased down in the saddle and turned in behind the cattle.

This time, the cattle did not break out in different directions, but they nevertheless ran as soon as they could make out the riders closing in from the north and the west. They did not race for it as they probably had done earlier, but they ran at a fair speed and covered considerable ground.

No one pushed them. When Tom Cartland came close

81

enough to make out the faces of the three youthful Cannons, it pleased him that, squatters or not, the Cannons seemed to know enough not to bust out in a rush behind the frightened cattle.

Everything went off as it was supposed to; the cattle eventually slackened pace a little, when they were convinced those riders back yonder were not going to race after them, and by the time Tom and the three young Cannons came together on their ride towards the home-place, the cattle were well away from Hartman's horse range.

The eldest son was a bearded, massive man like his father, but half a head taller, and he chewed tobacco. When he got up beside Tom he grinned through his beard and said, " I guess they figured we had an experienced drover with us this time, Sheriff."

Tom smiled back. " Naw; they were just plumb run down." He looked back. " Aren't there some more?"

" A few head," agreed the whiskered younger man. " But we can find them in the morning, if they don't pick up the scent and come on home by theirselves." One of the other men lifted his hat to vigorously scratch, then as he lowered the hat he said, " I'd sure like to know why anyone would run those darned cattle. Wouldn't have been none of Hartman's crew because they'd have run them *off* the horse range, not deeper across it. And there isn't anyone else up through here."

Jess said, " Maybe pot-hunters from Dennison, or maybe trappers comin' down from the mountains after a long winter."

"I'd like to have seen them doing that," stated the bearded elder son of George Cannon. "Critters don't have much tallow on 'em as it is, and them fellers tryin' to run that off." He looked at Cartland. "You heard of fellers being back through the mountains, Sheriff?"

Tom hadn't. He assumed the elder son meant renegades or fugitives so he said, "The Dennison Mountains been a hiding place for outlaws ever since I've been around here —and a heap longer than that from what folks have told me. But lately I haven't heard of anyone in particular being back up in there. Usually, the cowmen don't let their cattle go up there because of the lions and bears. Otherwise, if you settlers don't use the mountains either, most likely outlaws would get to settling in back up through there."

"Why would some come out and chouse our cattle?" asked Jess, and Tom Cartland had no answer.

"Lookin' for a fat yearling maybe, to make camp-meat out of. Darned if I know. Anyway, looks like the cattle are close enough to your claim now." Tom pointed; the cattle were back in familiar territory again and were spreading out now, for the most part over their fright and their excitement.

Jess rode for a short distance twisted in the saddle while he studied the distant, afternoon-shadowed far forested sidehills. As he sighed, finally, and faced forward again he said, "Well, they sure as hell seen the four of us, and that had ought to let 'em know they'd better not look for their camp-meat among our cattle again."

No one commented on that. Maybe the older sons of

George Cannon looked upon it as did Tom Cartland: if those renegades in the mountains really existed, and really were in need of camp-beef, the sight of four horsemen probably would not deter them at all. It would just make them almighty careful in the future.

When they reached the yard George was out front scrubbing off in a big wooden tub. Cartland's reshod black horse was sleepily standing in late-day warmth. George turned, waved, then boomed out an enquiry in a foghorn voice, and one of his sons called back just as thunderously that they had fetched back most of the critters and in the morning would fetch back the others.

Jess took the buckskin from Tom Cartland and led it away behind his brothers, who were also heading barnward to look after their animals. Cartland strolled over peeling off roping gloves and the moment he dug into a trouser pocket, George Cannon came out from behind his floursack towel with a dark look and a growl.

"No charge, Sheriff. Us folks need money, but we never need it *this* bad. You been a friend and a helper today."

Tom considered the older man, decided George meant exactly what he said, pulled the hand from his pocket and smiled. " I'm sure obliged to you. It's as good a resetting job as I've ever seen." He looked skyward. The day was nearly spent. It was time he headed back for town.

9

BLOOD IN THE GRASS

While Tom Cartland headed down across the lower foothills in the general direction of town he reflected that one
of the easiest, almost automatic, things a man could do was
make a comprehensive judgement of classes or tribes of
folks, such as all squatters or all freighters or all cattlemen
or all redskins.

Another aspect of this kind of thing was a man's heritage
or background. Tom Cartland had been a rangeman all his
adult life. People who were not range-bred or range-raised
aroused in him an awareness of the difference which existed
between his kind and their kind.

It was very easy to fall into that trap; if people dressed
differently, as squatters did, or lived differently, as the redskins did, his range-bred perceptiveness made him suspicious
of them.

Now, a mile down out of the rougher foothills where
those squatters had their hard-scrabble homesteads, he had
to face his prejudice because on the ride back he kept thinking of the Cannons, who were rough men, hard-working,
honest and strong-willed.

His prejudice considered all squatters to be like Will

O'Grady, and as a matter of fact many *were* like that. But not all, he told himself—by a darned sight not all of them.

Men like the Cannons were no different from rangemen in the ways that mattered. The fact that they had arrived late on the frontier and were putting down roots in land the stockmen had been using as though they owned it for the past generation or so, was basically why they were disliked—even fiercely hated by some rangemen—but Tom Cartland had sound instincts and one of them had told him a couple of years back that this initial wave of squatters was simply the beginning of something which would eventually take up so much land the rangeman's way of life would be inevitably altered.

He had resisted that idea too; like every man whose world had been an endless high sky and grasslands which ran out to the farthest curve of the horizon, Tom Cartland did not want change.

Now, turning all this over and over in his mind, he groped towards a solution which was perhaps unavoidable providing a man had an open mind. The change was coming, and that was all there was to it. He could not delay it and neither could any other rangeman. Also, disliking squatters was not going to make them depart. Like it or not, his world was going through a transition which would sadden him, but on the other hand moping wouldn't help, and beginning to appreciate men like George Cannon and his stalwart sons *would* help.

It would help him through the difficult phase of personal

change, without which he was going to be another of those old mossback-stockmen who would never relent, and who would be swamped by the very tides of change they disliked the most.

He was slouching along sorting out his thoughts on this topic, feeling his way towards some conclusions which would alleviate his decades-old prejudice, and did not hear horses until his saddle-mount changed leads as it tried to swing its head to look rearward.

He was raising up in the stirrups to twist from the waist and look back when the first gunshot erupted, and while it surprised him, it did even more for his horse; the animal gave a little forward jump as though it had been stung in the rear, then fought the bit as Tom instinctively tried to regain control, but he only tried to restrain the horse for a moment before he realised he had been the target of that gunman back yonder, then he leaned a little, let the reins run slack, and now when he turned he was bleak-eyed and confident. His black horse was one of the fastest saddle-animals in Dennison County.

Those men back yonder, three of them, were straining to close the distance. He finally had a good look at them. They were strangers to him. They were not squatters, they were rangemen, and they were now beginning to fall back as his black gelding settled into a belly-down run.

One of those men tried a one-handed shot with his carbine, which was bound to miss, and it did in fact go so far off Tom did not even sense danger.

For the first mile he had no time to speculate about

those men, but when he was passing beyond even saddlegun range, he eased up a little, veered slightly to his right which would allow him a better sighting of those pursuers back there a mile or more, and try to imagine why they had attacked him.

Initially, it had crossed his mind that they were the three younger Cannons. But that notion had died almost as it had been born. For one thing those men back yonder were well-mounted. For another thing they were obviously rangemen; they were even attired as rangemen.

They were strangers. He intently studied both men and horses before deciding he did not know them. Maybe they knew him; it was possible; a lot of cowboys, horse-hunters and other rangemen passed through Dennison. Many had earned a rebuke or worse from the sheriff. Usually on a Saturday night. He simply could not recall anyone he had roughed up enough to earn this kind of savage enmity. But a lawman never knew; sometimes the quietest kind were the most vindictively deadly.

One thing he could determine even as the distance steadily widened between him and his fierce pursuers; they all had guns in their fists and they wanted to kill him. Normally, men did not get into that kind of a mood over anything very trivial.

They hauled back, finally, slackening their pursuit since obviously they were not going to be able to overtake him, so he also drew up to a little slow lope, and eventually dropped down to a steady walk which would give his black horse a needed breather.

The trio of strangers seemed to either halt, back there in the distance, or to drop down to a slogging walk. Then a landswell intervened, Tom saw them no more, faced forward in the saddle to assess his position and decided he had covered a couple more miles riding westerly than he'd perhaps had to cover, so he reined back to his left in order to correct his course and still be on his way to town.

Evening was not far off, the sun was down and red and huge. Below it stood some saw-teeth mountain ridges, and down the near side of those distant slopes there was a haze like smoke which blurred upthrusts and smoothed out jagged lines upon the mountainsides until all that far-off primeval vastness looked almost tame and gentled.

Cartland, with no expectation of reaching town before dark, turned over in his mind the notion of making up a small posse of townsmen and heading back up in this area to search for the camp of those gun-handy strangers.

It would have been easy to overlook the episode, particularly since he had not been injured, and perhaps if he had not been a lawman he would have done this, but as he poked along—pausing now and then to listen, just in case— he decided those three strangers needed a lesson about indiscriminately attacking people.

He heard the evening stage coming down from the north where the road angled through the easterly foothills and made the crossing, finally, about eight miles distant where there was a wide, low pass through the Dennison Mountains.

Otherwise, the dusk was still, and deceptively mild, and hushed.

The lights of town were distantly visible by the time he had crossed towards the coachroad. The smell of dust was noticeable, in the wake of that stagecoach, but there was no other traffic as he came down across a graded shoulder and reached the thoroughfare itself where he turned directly southward without any inkling of impending disaster.

He had from time to time paused to stand in the stirrups, look and listen, then sit down and ride on again. He had very expertly outridden his pursuers so there was no reason to anticipate any difficulty. Also, he was getting steadily closer to town, so when the spiteful flat report of a carbine being fired ahead and to his left, over along the east side of the road somewhere not too distant, shattered his world of silent safety, he reacted with momentary paralysed astonishment, then he yanked his horse to the left, drew and fired his Colt where he thought that hidden rifleman had been.

And, of course, the hidden rifleman was no longer there.

The carbine held off as though the man behind it over yonder somewhere in the dark of the easterly range was waiting for something to tell him exactly where Sheriff Cartland was. Of course he got that when the black horse was reined away and rattled roadway gravel under his freshly reset shoes. The carbine's owner fired on a tangent with his gunbarrel slightly tilted. This time Tom felt the bullet and dropped down the far side of his horse, trying to twist and fire back but it was useless so he waited, cocked gun ready, but did not tug the trigger.

It just did not seem possible that this attacker was one of those three strangers from miles back, and yet it was pushing coincidence quite a ways to expect this to be some-one totally different who also happened to select this parti-cular day to want to assassinate Sheriff Tom Cartland.

His black horse was stretching wide to leave the roadway and jump across the low little roadway-burn when the gun-man cut loose for the last time. Tom saw the muzzleblast which he had not been able to locate before, and with his gun ready, he fired only a second or two after the carbine had lanced the night with red-orange flame.

A man suddenly cried out, then full silence resettled on all sides as Cartland pulled up on the black and sat a long while looking back and listening.

There was no more gunfire. There was no noise over there either, but then there had never been any noise from the area of that hidden bushwhacker.

Tom swung down from the saddle, stood on the far side of his horse for a long while trying to make up his mind whether that cry had been a deliberate attempt to lure him back into the killer's sights or not, and in the end decided it was equally as possible—even *more* possible—that he had shot his ambusher. He knew for a fact that he had drilled that .45 slug directly down into the centre of the muzzle-blast. Maybe that had been a pure stroke of luck, but whatever it was he had done it and now he started back, pulling the horse behind him.

At the edge of the roadway he paused again. Those two old smelly juniper trees where the O'Grady lad had initially found the dead man, were close by, but not close enough for him to walk over and tether his horse among them. On the other hand there was no way to keep the horse from making noise when it got back upon the roadway gravel.

He looked down in the direction of town, sighed because he knew the moment he relinquished the reins he would be afoot, then he let the reins slide through his fingers anyway; better to have to walk two or three miles than to have the horse draw gunfire towards them both perhaps with fatal results.

He stepped down into the roadway and when the horse would have followed he flagged with both arms and the horse threw up its head, halted, then stood looking after him as he started onward. Any other time the horse would have turned and made a bee-line for home. This time, he simply stood there.

Cartland got fully across the road and up onto the rougher land on the east side of it. He was becoming increasingly confident he had indeed shot his ambusher. Even so he was by nature a prudent individual—which this time at any rate kept him alive, because when he was less than fifty yards from the spot where he had fired into the muzzle-blast, booted feet abruptly dug in as a man spun towards him in the darkness, evidently having either detected shadowy movement or having discerned stealthy sounds, and the startled individual did exactly what Tom Cartland would have done, he fired, cocked his Colt and fired again.

The first sound-shot went wild. The second one did not go wild.

Tom had a sensation of great heat spiralling upwards

from deep inside him somewhere, then he felt as though he were plunging headlong down a black tunnel and that was all.

Those two sixgun blasts sounded extremely loud in the dark hush of advancing nightfall. Without any doubt down in Dennison people had heard them, and this may have been what motivated the sinewy, lanky man who had fired them to hasten over where he had seen that silhouette go down without a sound, and to stand over the face-down lawman with his gun cocked, until a second man strode up, nudged the downed man with a boot-toe and said. " That's the end of Dan Brady—the son of a bitch." Then this second man turned on his heel to return to the spot where he and his friend had been kneeling beside a third man when Tom Cartland had been shot.

The lanky man holstered his Colt, sank to one knee, rolled Cartland over and remained utterly still when he saw reflected starlight off a lawman's badge. Finally he said, " Hey, Bert, this here ain't Dan, it's a lawman."

When there was no response from behind him the lanky man started groping through Tom Cartland's pockets. He stopped and hauled back when he had the engraved gold watch in his hand. He turned it over and over, flipped open the front, flipped open the back, then closed the case and gazed perplexedly at the still grey face of the man on the ground in front of him. Finally, without raising his voice he said, " Bert, come over here for a minute."

Bert's answer was harsh. " Didn't you see how bad Earl was hit? The hell with that idiot!"

As though he had not been rebuked, and while he was still staring at Tom Cartland the sinewy man tried again by saying, " You better come over here. We come one hell of a long way for what I got in my hand—and the rest of it."

The squatting man arose, cursing to himself, went over and looked as the sinewy man held up his palm with the engraved gold watch on it.

Bert stopped in his tracks, stared, then snatched at the watch and held it up close while he looked it over very carefully.

" Look inside the front of the case," said the sinewy man. " Old Kildare's initials is in there just like they is on all those gawddamn J L K cattle and horses. Open it."

Bert obeyed, saw the initials, looked down at Tom, then sounded puzzled when he said, " How'n hell did this feller get it, Curtis?"

The sinewy man replied dryly. " I got no idea how he got that watch, but if he got *that*, then I'll lay you odds he had some other stuff from Dan in his saddlebags, and maybe he even had the damned moneybelt."

" But hell—this was supposed to be Dan. You seen him riding his lousy buckskin horse the same as Earl and I did back yonder with them other fellers when they set out to gather up them darned cattle we tried to get a shot at. That was Dan Brady, you said so yourself; that was his horse and his . . ."

" I also said it was a hell of a long ways to make a positive identification, if you'll remember."

94

"But we all recognised his buckskin horse, damn it all."

Curtis shifted position, stood hipshot with thumbs hooked in his shellbelt and said, "Something's bad wrong, I can see that. This ain't Dan like we figured when we tried to kill the bastard. But this here lawman's got the Kildare watch and he sure as the devil was riding Dan Brady's buckskin horse . . . Bert; I'll lay you odds this here lawman somehow or other grabbed Dan, likely enough got him locked up in his jailhouse, and if he done *that*, you know darned well where the moneybelt is—in this lawman's safe, or at least in some safe down in that town we seen when we first come into this country . . . Our money, by gawd!"

The wounded man groaned. Bert and Curtis turned slightly, but with a lot less interest than they had shown earlier, then Bert said, "Earl's not going to make it. That was one hell of a lucky shot by this lawman. Right through the lights, high up and near the centre. He ain't going to make it." Bert turned his back on the dying man and gazed coldly at Cartland. "How about him, where did I hit him?"

Curtis also turned to look down. "Didn't look," he muttered. "After I found the watch I didn't look no further. But I think you either shot him in the head or alongside it. There's plenty of blood on the grass up there."

10

IN THE DARK

Neither of those dark-night wraiths got a chance to lean and examine Tom Cartland. Into the southward silence came a steadily increasing sound of horsemen and it did not sound as though it were only one or two of them either.

Bert dropped the Kildare watch into a pocket, looked around as he said, " Where is this feller's black horse?" then speedily abandoned whatever idea he might have had of finding Cartland's animal as the sound of horsemen grew louder. " Come on," he said swiftly. " Let's get the hell out of here."

They hastened away on foot, travelling north-easterly. Behind, back where they had been, and a little farther, back in the direction of town, a man's rough voice sang out.

" There's Sheriff Cartland's black gelding!"

Riders hauled down to a sliding halt, looked left and right, and when two riders peeled off to catch the gelding another man in the clutch of townsmen spoke up, and this time the voice was grumpy as well as sceptical.

" This is asinine. For all we know whatever happened didn't even occur around here. Those gunshots could have come from a mile in any other direction."

The man who had made this complaining statement eased his animal up over the roadside-burn and let the beast poke ahead a few yards, then cursed when the animal suddenly dug in with all four feet and snorted, head lowered and ears pointing.

Another rider came up, looked, swung off without a word and stood at the head of his mount as he stared. " It's the sheriff," he said quietly, as though he and the complaining man were the only ones out there. Then he raised his voice. " Hey, over here, it's Tom Cartland! Doc, get down and look at him."

Doc Bannon had already swung to earth. He went up and sank to his knees, studied the inert figure, then shoved back his old hat and leaned with both hands outstretched. Around him the others came over to the east side of the stageroad. They muttered, asked questions, and finally stood around in strong silence while Doctor Bannon completed his examination and leaned back to glance up.

" Someone had best ride to town and fetch back a wagon. And pitch some hay into the bed. And don't get some darned old squatter-outfit with no springs under it."

Brutus Tolbert leaned from the hips. " He ain't dead, then?"

Doctor Bannon looked at the liveryman. " Hate to disappoint you," he growled sarcastically. " Brutus, you got some wagons. How about you riding back to town to bring one up here?"

Tolbert nodded and turned away with his horse in tow

without another word. Amos Jennings, the vinegary store-clerk, and his employer Abe Markham, crowded ahead and gazed downward. Amos, who rarely saw any good in anything, said, "Dyin' ain't he, Doctor?"

Bannon was annoyed. "No, he's not dying. He's got a mean gouge up alongside the head in the hair, and he'll have a scar there until he learns how to comb his hair to cover it, but otherwise I'd say—barring a concussion—he'd ought to be up and around again shortly."

Abe Markham turned away. "Whoever shot him might still be out there."

The clerk, his employer, and two other townsmen moved off, cautiously and as silently as they could, but without making much real effort to flush out a gunman or two.

Doc sighed, dug out a small black cigar, lighted it and continued to sit there on his heels gazing at the injured lawman. He had not been taken entirely in Cartland's confidence, but neither was he a fool. Some men had excellent powers of deduction. Actually, that, as much as anything else was what determined a good doctor from a poor one, and Joshua Bannon was a good diagnostician, so now he turned that capability to this present predicament and decided that Tom Cartland had most likely been shot by someone involved in the killing of that John Doe cowboy. It only required another few thoughtful pulls on the Mex stogie for him to also decide that whoever had shot the sheriff, and who was involved in that other, more lethal shooting, was probably motivated by six thousand dollars in a sweat-stained moneybelt.

He said, "You always did stick your head up like a ferret, Sheriff. Maybe this time you'll learn to keep it down and let the other feller show himself."

Doc got up to his feet, with a grimace, rubbed his knees for a moment and turned to listen to the calls his companions were making out yonder as they reluctantly scouted up the night. Doc smiled, spat, plugged the cigar back between his teeth, and shook his head. Those gunmen were not out there. No gunman worth his salt would have dallied after shooting a county sheriff. Not in cow-country anyway where people were likely to say little, and get about an efficient lynching without much delay.

Abe Markham returned, leading his horse. "Nothing out there," he reported, as though Doc were their leader. Doc merely shrugged, as Markham looked down. "Sure he'll make it are you, Joshua?"

Doc sniffed. "Thirty years ago I learned never to give a direct answer to that darned question. Of course I'm not sure. Do I look like God?"

Markham sombrely gazed at Doc. "No," he replied, "you sure as hell don't . . . Well, what do you expect this was all about? It sounded like a regular blessed war, when I heard the shootin' down in town. Sounded like maybe six or eight fellers was out here goin' at it hammer and tongs."

Doc did not have to answer the question because Jennings and two other townsmen straggled back. The two men with Markham's clerk announced that not only was there no sign of gunmen out yonder, but as long as everything seemed to have been settled, they would head on back to town. They took Barney Shannon the saloonman back with them. If Barney had not been caught up in the excitement he never would have left his bar in the care of a substitute bartender to come charging out here in the first place. Ordinarily, Barney stayed in town, minded his own business and operated his successful and lucrative saloon.

When Barney and the others had departed Amos Jennings sniffed and suggested to Abe Markham that they might as well head back too. Abe responded by telling his clerk to go back; there was no need for him to remain out here anyway, but that he would stay with Doc until Brutus got back with the wagon.

Amos loped away, elbows flopping in the night as he galloped in his own inimitable and ungainly style after the other departing townsmen.

Abe said, "I got to tell you, Joshua, this darned country'll never be the same, now that the settlers are coming in. Folks being shot right out of their saddles when they're peacefully riding down the road at night. It's a darned pity, that's what it is."

Doc smoked and considered Sheriff Cartland almost casually, and after a while he turned aside to expectorate again, turned back and said, "Whoever shot him, Abe, went through his pockets. Pulled the cloth inside out—see there."

"I'll be damned," exclaimed Markham, looking closely at Cartland. "Highwaymen!"

Doc was mildly sceptical. "You think so, do you?"

" Well, of course it was highwaymen."

" Then why in hell didn't they stop the stagecoach which came down through here a few minutes before they shot Tom Cartland? If there were two or three of them, which is what it sounded like, they would have been able to halt the coach, and they certainly could have expected to do better robbing a stage than just a solitary lawman riding down the road, wouldn't you imagine?"

Markham tugged at his beard. " Then who was it; someone with a grudge? Some cowboy Tom tossed into his cells some Saturday night?"

Doc did not commit himself. He bent to gaze into the grey face of the unconscious lawman, puffed a while, then straightened back and spat out his smoked-down stogie. " He'll be able to tell us something—maybe not all of it but some of it—when he comes around . . . What in tarnation is taking Brutus so long?"

" He's on his way," stated Markham. " I caught the sound of a wagon over stones a while back. Listen."

Bannon heard, blew out a rough breath and said, " Abe, those gunmen or whatever they were are still out there. Not close by, but they didn't just stand up and shoot it out with Tom because they wanted to rob a man, then fled out of the country. I'm satisfied there's more to this than just someone gettin' shot."

Markham pondered, and during that interval of time the sound of a team hauling an empty wagon that rattled over hard ground with each turn of the wheels got increasingly louder. Then Abe said, " We still got the township vigilantes, Doc. The sheriff thinks we disbanded but we never did, and maybe now it'll turn out for the best that we didn't. If someone comes around lookin' for trouble, we can darned well handle it, I expect."

The wagon and hitch hove into sight with darkness all around. Doctor Bannon watched it and made no comment upon Abe Markham's statement. Doc, too, had no use for township vigilantes.

Tolbert pulled down to a fast walk for the last hundred yards or so, saw Markham and Doctor Bannon and edged his hitch and wagon right up to the right-hand side of the road, kicked on his binders, looped the lines round the brake-handle and called over as he started to climb down.

"Sure stirred up a hornet's nest in town when folks learnt it was Sheriff Cartland got shot. They're madder'n a coop full of wet hens."

Doc was not interested. It was getting cold and it was also getting late, he'd had a long day and right now he simply wanted to return to his cottage, to the stove, and maybe to a pot of Irish coffee and some quiet reflection, so he said, "Lend a hand, Brutus. Did you pitch some hay in the wagon?"

"Straw, Doc, straw. Hay costs money. Yeah, I put some straw in."

They were careful about lifting the lawman and easing him into the back of the old drayage wagon atop the dry-smelling yellow straw. As an afterthought Brutus said, "You fellers know if Sheriff Cartland's got hay fever?"

Neither Markham nor Bannon answered. Doc gestured.

"Get up on the seat, Brutus, and head back." He turned, stepped clear, watched the liveryman make a big full-scale turn, then he and Abe went after their saddlehorses, Doc rubbing his hands together briskly.

Tolbert had certainly told the truth. Late as it now was, when the wagon and its slouching escort appeared back down in town people came forth to look into the wagon, emptying both the poolhall and the saloon. Doctor Bannon thought there also had to be people fresh from their warm beds. Otherwise it did not make much sense to believe all those onlookers had still been stirring at this late hour.

When men shouted questions to him Doc answered candidly by saying that until he could make a thorough examination in decent light at his clinic he would not know the full extent of Sheriff Cartland's injuries.

He repeated that four times and was about to say it again when Brutus tooled his hitch over to the duckboards in front of Doc's cottage, when Pocho the hostler from the stage company's corralyard shouldered through and called to Doc offering to help carry Cartland inside. Doc nodded assent, dismounted, handed his reins to Abe Markham, and supervised the lifting and carrying of the lawman.

Once inside with just the cock-eyed corralyard-hostler beside the bed where they had placed Tom Cartland, Doc yawned, peeled off his hat and coat, yawned again and turned to say, "You any good at tracking?"

Pocho's good eye settled darkly upon Doc. He said nothing until the other eye came somewhat aimlessly on around and got into position to also stare at the medical practitioner, then Pocho said, " *Si.* I can read sign right good. Why?"

" Tomorrow, then, before all the idiots from town rush up there, back-track the wagon to the place where Tom Cartland was shot, and see if you can't pick up the sign of the men who shot him. See where it leads to and what you can make of it . . . I'll pay you."

Pocho's good eye went to the grey-faced, bloody man on the bed. " No, you don't pay me," he said quietly. " *Jefe* and I are friends."

Doc said, " All right. Now get out of here, I've got work to do."

The Mexican left, hat in hand. Out front on the little porch he paused to purse his lips and cast a narrowed gaze northward. He had noticed a detail back in there—the sheriff's pockets had been pulled out a little where someone had rummaged through them.

To Pocho that simply meant robbers had jumped a traveller from beside the road in the dark. It did not mean they had known they were attacking the county sheriff.

He shrugged, crushed on his old hat and started southward in the direction of the corralyard bunkhouse. He would track those men; not expecting to find them, and not convinced they were anything but common night-time thieves.

Over along Barney Shannon's bar townsmen and a few rangemen were discussing this affair and were arriving at the identical conclusion : it had simply been an attack on a traveller by nocturnal highwaymen.

11

SHERLOCK WHO?

Joshua Bannon kept bad hours. Being a single man who lived alone—most of the time anyway; whenever he did not have an ill person in his combination residence-hospital —he retired when he felt like it, arose when he could not sleep, and generally obeyed the dictates of a personal nature which was totally independent.

He made some coffee after cleaning up Sheriff Cartland, poured a little sourmash whisky into it, heated some water on his kitchen stove to wash and shave by, and rolled his collar under after dispensing with his hat and coat, sipped laced coffee and shaved and scrubbed. It was past midnight before he was finished. There were no lights along Main Street excluding the pair of smoking old carriage lamps down at the livery barn, one on each side of the big doorless front opening.

Otherwise, barring the residence of the local plumber whose children—all three of them—had taken the whooping cough, the residential area of Dennison was also darkened.

Doc fried some meat and potatoes, ate them, washed up his kitchen and lit a cigar as he stood by a front-wall window looking out over the dark town. He was killing time, something he was adept at.

An hour later he filled a cup with his Irish coffee and took it to Tom Cartland's room, placed it atop a little table at bedside and was feeling through all his pockets for a cigar when the sheriff said, "Don't light one of those damned things in here unless you open the windows, Doc."

Bannon ended his search, picked up the coffee, wordlessly went over to hoist his patient and punch a rolled blanket in behind him, and to say, "You just swallow and I'll pour. If you don't swallow you'll drown. Now swallow!"

There was no question of Sheriff Cartland having a choice. He swallowed rapidly, until the cup had been drained, then he sighed and raised a hand to his bandaged head.

Bannon put aside the cup. "What do you remember?" he asked. "In case your memory needs jogging—you were shot up alongside the head. It looked a lot worse than it really was. Even so, you're going to have a scar up there. Now tell me what you can remember."

Tom gingerly explored the bandage before replying. "Three riders tried to overhaul me when I was coming down from the squatters' foothills. An hour or so later some son of a bitch ahead of me, and on the east side of the road, tried to bushwhack me. Right now I don't recollect much else, Doc."

"By any chance do you recall firing back? Because you —or someone, anyway—killed a man out there. Stranger to me."

Cartland looked blank. " Killed a man . . . ?"

Doc sighed. " Forget it for now."

Cartland faintly frowned. " If that was those same fellers who chased me from back near the foothills, how could they have got around me and on ahead? I outran them easy, back up there."

Doc had no reply so he said, " Pocho is going out to hunt for tracks and see what he can . . ."

" I'll be damned," blurted out the lawman. " That stage-coach. You mentioning Pocho reminded me—there was a stage went past towards town . . . Doc, do me a favour, go down to the corralyard and roust out the driver or gun-guard that was on that stage and ask them if three fellers stopped the stage north of town about four or five miles and rode it on down, then got off north of here—up where I got bushwhacked."

Bannon, with no intention at all of going down to the corralyard bunkhouse to awaken some slumbering stagers at two o'clock in the morning, stood there wagging his head. " In the morning. In the morning," he exclaimed. " Right now let's sort things out a little, Tom. In the first place, it don't look to me as though someone was out to rob you even though they went through your pockets."

Cartland said, " Damn it—the watch! Doc, was there a gold watch on me when you came up there?"

Bannon, nor anyone else, had searched the sheriff, which is what the medical practitioner now said, so Sheriff Cart-land insisted that Doc make the search now, and of course, there was no gold watch. But perhaps significantly, nothing else which had been in Cartland's pockets, including a small sum of money, was missing.

After Sheriff Cartland had explained about the watch, where he got it and what was important about it—those initials inside the front cover—Doctor Bannon went thoughtfully rummaging through his pockets in search of a cigar which was not there and which he had forgotten that he'd searched for earlier, and when he was ready to abandon this hunt he said, " Right from the time we come onto you last night, Tom, I been thinking your shooting likely had something to do with that dead cowboy and that six thousand dollars. Now it's beginning to look to me as though someone had a reason for taking just that gold watch off you, and not also cleaning you out down to your spurs and gun. Who was J L K?"

" A rancher over around Casa Verde. We already discussed that, Doc, and you said you'd been in Casa Verde."

" I didn't mean who *exactly* was J L K, sonny, I meant what was his connection with three—four counting that John Doe feller we buried—what was his connection with four gun-handy individuals?"

" They robbed him," replied Tom Cartland. " That's my guess. Maybe they also killed him. Otherwise, if he was a big cowman, why would he be associating with men who'd take a watch off him and maybe even his moneybelt?"

" Fine," conceded Doctor Bannon. " Now we're getting down to it."

" To what?"

Doc benignly smiled in the direction of the man in the

bed. " Bannon's law, sonny."

Sheriff Cartland looked annoyedly at the older man. " Have you been drinking tonight, Doc?"

Bannon continued to wear that benign small smile as he explained. " Years back I worked this out. Generally speaking the male human bodies consists by weight of sixty-six pounds of muscle and three pounds of brain. Does that tell you anything? Well, let me put it this way, Sheriff: Bannon's law says that any time an animal has a lot of brawn and a little brain, it is going to be a forceful, dim-witted, obnoxious and troublesome critter. That's Bannon's law. You understand, do you?"

Tom leaned against the rolled-up blanket which was supporting his upper body and gazed steadily at Joshua Bannon for a silent long moment, then he reached for the cup with the lukewarm Irish coffee, and drained it, then put aside the cup and started to ease around so that he could punch that blanket from behind himself and get composed for some rest.

" You *have* been drinking," he growled. " Go to bed, Doc."

Bannon in fact did leave the room, but to go in search of a stogie. Even so, after he had located one and had lighted it, he did not return to the sick-room, but went ambling out to the kitchen for another cup of coffee—laced with sourmash liquor—and, trailing the acrid aroma of his cigar and carefully carrying the cup of coffee he went off to his own quarters, lighted a lamp in there, got ready for bed, finished the coffee and put aside the cigar, climbed inside his clammy muslin sheets and lay back in darkness turning a number of seemingly poorly-related events and facts over and over in his mind.

When sleep finally came, Doc was as ready for it as he would one day be ready for a more permanent variety of sleep. He was not a man lacking in imagination or anxieties, he was, however, an individual with a singular lack of deep concern about himself, or his future, and the reason for that was simple enough : Doc had witnessed his share of passings in his lifetime, and whatever death presaged, one thing was a dead certainty. He would not have to be the first to pioneer that trail, meaning that it had been damned well blazed by an awful lot of folks who had preceded him, and that took a lot of the worry out of it for him. In fact a lot of Doc's oldest and best friends had gone on ahead. He should have no trouble finding the trail nor staying on it.

As for Bannon's law, that was the basis for Doc's private philosophy, and whether Tom Cartland had looked disgustedly at him or not Doc remained as convinced tonight as he had been thirty years back when he had first worked out his law, that it was absolutely correct.

So he slept, finally, with a clear conscience—well, at least with a relatively clear conscience—and when he awakened with the sun blazing through a window directly into his eyes, he greeted the magnificent new springtime day with a sound curse, tried to hide from the sunlight, had to give it up eventually and to arise.

By the time he was ready to enter the sick-room and arouse the sheriff, Tom Cartland was already up and dressed and puttering in Doc's kitchen trying to coax fire under the coffeepot. When Doc entered and looked over there, Tom said, " Did you ever hear of cleaning the ashes out of the firebox? How do you get a fire going in this blasted stove when there's ash right up to the top of the burners?"

Doc accepted the rebuke without comment, went over, kicked the side of the stove vigorously several times until some of the topmost ash settled lower, then he shouldered his guest aside and kindled a little fire as he said, " Trouble with you young fellers is that everything's got to be just so. Now, when you get old enough to accept the way of things and not fight against everything, you'll be on the way to acquiring real wisdom ... By the way, it came to me last night that all we got to do is find a man packing the J L K watch and we'll have all the answers to our riddle ... Do you like hoecakes for breakfast?"

Cartland went to a chair and sat at the kitchen table as he said, " Just coffee, thanks. Did you put medicine in that coffee last night? I never slept so well in my life and this morning there is almost no headache."

Doc had put in nothing but whisky, but he was well-versed in his profession, so he acting all-knowing and wise as he said, " Sonny, just because a man practises his ancient and exalted art of healing in a cow-town don't have to mean he isn't proficient at his trade. Just be grateful you got me for your doctor ... You want anything in this coffee?"

" Just black. And tell me something, oh exalted proficient pill-roller—just how do I find this feller packing the gold watch?"

"Set down beside your safe, sonny, and wait. If he knows that watch, then he damned well also knows there is a moneybelt stuffed with greenbacks somewhere around here, and if he and his friends—excluding the one we planted in the graveyard—came all the way from Arizona to find that moneybelt, don't think just shooting you is going to slow them down very much. It may make them careful as hell, but it's not going to keep them away. It wouldn't keep *me* away if I was an outlaw and knew there was six thousand dollars somewhere close by. Would it you?"

Tom did not get a chance to reply, someone out front banging insistently on the roadside door made Doc hasten away muttering under his breath about injured people not having enough consideration to wait until after he'd eaten to start pestering him with their blasted ailments. Then it turned out not to be a patient, but rather Brutus Tolbert, who barely allowed Doctor Bannon to get the door open before he said, "If the sheriff's still here he might like to know his darned black horse was out back of my barn come daylight eatin' off my haystack." Then Brutus lowered his voice a little. "And that dead feller from up yonder—we brought him in this morning early and put him on the table across the alley in your wagon-shed, Doc." Brutus held forth a heavy blue bandanna which was knotted at the top. "All his gatherings is in here, Doc, so you can give 'em to the sheriff—except four bits which I taken out, considering I had that much coming for going back out there and fetching in the carcass this morning. That's what I'd normally charge."

Bannon accepted the heavy bandanna. "What's in here —lead?"

"Two guns, Doc. One was that feller's sixshooter. It's been fired a couple of times, then there's one of those nasty little under-and-over belly-guns, small calibre but solid steel. By the way—how is the sheriff?"

"Doing right well, and he'll be pleased to know you were concerned, Brutus. Anything else?"

"No, I was just wondering . . ."

"Thanks for coming by," said Bannon, and closed the door. When he returned to the kitchen Tom had got his own coffee, and gazed dispassionately at the blue bandanna Doc put on the table in front of him.

Doc explained who the caller had been and what was wrapped up in the blue bandanna as he leaned to loosen the knots and paw through the personal things until he had the little derringer in his fist. Then he studied it closely before smiling triumphantly.

"That's what I was looking for," he exclaimed, and pushed the little weapon towards Sheriff Cartland. "Thirty-one or thirty-two calibre, Tom. Same calibre as that bullet I dug out of the cowboy we buried. Now I think we can figure what happened. I thought it had to be something like this when I dug that slug out. This man you shot last night—or someone shot anyway and I think it had to be you since I doubt if his friends was shooting at him— this feller and his friends were chasing that John Doe cowboy—I'd say because he ran off with the moneybelt and all the money, plus the gold watch. The man who owned this belly-gun got off a lucky shot and hit the John Doe outlaw in the back. It took a while, but eventually the shot-feller sat down under that juniper tree to die."

Doc dropped the little gun in front of Cartland. " You can use this as evidence. I got to confide something in you, sonny. I always knew I'd have made a splendid detective. Did you ever read any of those stories about Sherlock Holmes?"

Tom looked up from the little gun. " Who?"

" Never mind. That's the trouble with spending all your darned life sleeping under the stars and staring at the rear end of a lot of stupid cattle. Anyway . . ."

" Whoa, Doc. Just a minute," said Cartland, arising with the blue bandanna and the little gun in his hands. " Is there any reason why I got to stay here? Am I fit enough to go on down to the jailhouse?"

" Go ahead," replied Bannon. " Go right ahead and as soon as I've finished breakfast and cleaned up the kitchen I'll be along and we can plan our next moves."

Sheriff Cartland looked over at the older man. " Sherlock Gomes?"

" *Holmes*, confound it. He was an Englishman not a Messican."

Tom Cartland turned on his heel heading back for the room where he'd spent the night to get his shellbelt, his holstered gun and his hat. Doc remembered something and called after him.

" Brutus has your black horse down at the livery barn!"

12

DEDUCTIVE POWERS

Abe Markham, and even Amos Jennings, the store-clerk with the unsmiling, vinegary face, along with several other townsmen such as Barney Shannon, the saloonman and Jim Bryan, the stage company's Dennison representative, stopped by as soon as it was rumoured up and down Main Street that Sheriff Cartland had been seen entering his office with a bandage under his hat. Everyone was relieved to learn that Cartland's injury had been no worse than it evidently was, and Brutus wanted two-bits for the hay the black gelding had consumed after having fed all night at Brutus's haystack.

Tom paid, then, remembering what Doc had told him about Pocho, asked if the cock-eyed hostler had been seen back in town and Brutus looked blank. "He don't work for me. You'd have to ask Jim Bryan. I wouldn't hire Pocho Ramirez to sweep my runway. I never employ boozers. By the way, there was some money in that blue bandanna which I didn't count nor anything, but if no one lays claim to that dead feller's effects, I'd like to . . ."

Cartland looked up. "Brutus, you are a man who is all heart," he said, then turned his back on the liveryman, who left the office a little pink in the face.

Among the things taken from the dead gunman and brought to town in the dead gunman's blue bandanna, aside from his sixgun and the derringer, was thirty-five dollars in greenbacks and some silver, a Barlow clasp-knife, some string wrapped in a tight little wad, some tobacco and cigarette papers, two keys and some sulphur matches to light cigarettes with.

Tom Cartland was not very impressed. He had hoped for a letter or at least something with some names on it, exactly as he had similarly hoped for something of that nature among the effects of the John Doe cowboy, but his disappointment was short-lived. Just ahead of high noon Pocho came ambling back into town astride a nice *grulla* gelding marked with the stage company's branch—W F—back-to-back. Pocho tied up out front, stood a moment gazing at the front of the jailhouse, then shrugged and stumped on over to push inside rolling his good eye around as he said, " It's hot work, riding all over like I been doing. Hot and dry work, *jefe*."

Cartland pretended to be sympathetic when he said, " Sit down and I'll fetch you some coffee."

Pocho sat, but his pock-marked, coarse features assumed an expression of inner pain as he said. " Not coffee, *jefe*. Especially not your coffee... You got any *cerbeza* in here?"

Tom shook his head. "Barney's bar," he replied, going over to ease down at the littered desk. " How much tracking did you do, Pocho, there was three of them?"

" Ah; you talked to Mister Bryan at the stage office."

" I didn't talk to anyone," explained Sheriff Cartland. " There was no other way those men could have got around me after I outran them back near the foothills. They flagged down the coach, rode it down ahead of me, piled off and set up their bushwhack."

" That's good," beamed Pocho Ramirez. " *Jefe*, that is very good—for a *corbacho*."

" For a what?"

" Never mind, *jefe*. Anyway, you guessed it exactly the way they done it. And after they shot you and run off, they was on foot so it wasn't real hard to shag them back a few miles to where they'd tied their horses when they'd flagged down the stage . . . There was three horses. One belonged to that feller you shot. Anyway, they clumb astride and headed towards the westerly foothills. Headed in the direction of those squatter homesteads. *Jefe*, that's all open country, you unnerstand. Well, if they didn't head right on up the pass to get the hell out of the territory after shootin' a sheriff, why then they figured to hide out in them hills, I figured, and if they done that, and here I come ridin' along trackin' them, and they was settin' back in the trees up yonder watching . . . What would *you* think if you seen me trackin' along like that?" Pocho slowly leaned, slowly simulated a man picking up his Winchester, snugging it back while he carefully tracked a mythical rider down his sights, then he pulled the trigger, rolled up his eyes and in Spanish said, " May I have died swiftly and in His grace." Then he rolled both his eyes, the good one and the bad one, back around to the lawman's face. " All right?"

It had to be all right since clearly Pocho knew no more than he had just related. Cartland fished for half a cart-wheel and spun it over the desk-top litter. "For *cerbeza*," he said, "and if Jim Bryan raises hell about you not being at work this morning . . ."

Pocho arose with the silver half-dollar in his hand. "He already knows where I been. I told him when I borrowed the company horse." Pocho went as far as the door then turned to also say, "*Jefe*, you want to know what I think? Anyone who'd go to all the sweat those fellers went to last night, just to get a couple of shots at you—they are goin' to try again as soon as they know they didn't kill you. Why? I don't know and it's none of my business. *Adios*."

After the corralyard-man's departure Sheriff Cartland went back to minutely examining the things from the blue bandanna. In the end he swept them all into a drawer and arose to ease the hat down atop his bandaged thatch and to go stand at a front-wall window gazing out into the drowsy, sun-drenched warm roadway.

He saw Jim Bryan across in front of the general store talking briskly to Pocho, and guessed Bryan was annoyed so he went out to cross over and intercede on the part of the hostler. But Pocho suddenly smiled, nodded and went walking up in the direction of Shannon's saloon, and when Bryan saw the sheriff heading his way he waited, then said, "Pocho just told me what he'd discovered. Looks like you got some personal enemies, Tom."

Cartland glanced past, up where the stocky Mexican was turning in at Barney's place. With someone like Pocho shooting off his mouth all over town nothing would be a secret for very long. He shrugged and swung his attention back to the stage company's local representative.

"I need some descriptions of those three fellers who flagged down the coach last night and got ahead to set up their ambush, Jim."

Bryan looked uncomfortable. "The driver and gunguard left out before dawn on a southbound stage, Tom. They got scheduled runs and you know how it is—we run a little short-handed now and then." Bryan held up both palms. "I talked to 'em both last night after we saw what had happened. Neither of them remembered any of those three fellers. The strangers said their horses got stampeded by a bear in some camp west of the road a couple miles through the foothills and they needed a ride down to town where they could rent more horses to go back and hunt their critters with . . . Then, when the coach got down to the corralyard, those three fellers wasn't on it. That's the whole story, Tom. My boys said they couldn't even say whether those was young men or old ones in the dark, and them bein' in a hurry to get to town and all. I'm sorry as hell."

Abe Markham came out and stood in front of his roadway window gazing over where Bryan and Cartland were talking. When he caught the lawman's eye he held up three envelopes. Evidently the morning mail had arrived and had already been sorted. Tom smiled at Jim Bryan and turned away to walk up and take the letters from Abe.

Markham said, "It's a darned relief to see you moving

around again. Last night up there in the dark you didn't look worth a darn."

"Didn't feel worth a darn," murmured the sheriff and added a little more. "Thanks for the mail, Abe."

He struck out again for his office across the road, got inside before he opened the letters, and one of them had a freshly-printed fugitive-dodger in it. No letter or anything else, just that slightly stiff, newly printed and freshly-folded wanted dodger in it.

The picture was of that John Doe cowboy. It was unmistakably him. The name below it was given as 'Daniel Leary Brady' and he was wanted for robbery and murder over in Arizona, in two places, Indian Wells and Casa Verde. His physical description was given; it matched perfectly. The description was followed by a list of criminal violations going back seven years. Daniel Leary Brady had been a thoroughgoing outlaw; clearly an incorrigible one, and he had last been a member of an outlaw band known as the Feldon Gang.

What Cartland looked for and never found was a detailed outline of the crimes Brady had been involved in over around Casa Verde. He had already fairly well made up his mind about the extent of that involvement, and about the variety of the crimes, but he needed more than his personal guesswork.

He did not get it; the dodger did not define any of the crimes around either Indian Wells nor Casa Verde which Dan Brady had participated in although it cryptically defined a whole series of earlier crimes.

120

Cartland tossed down the dodger in disgust, just as the office door opened and Doctor Bannon walked in. Being a practised observer Doc saw that wanted poster immediately, recognised the face-view picture on it and stepped across to the desk to look down, as he said, " I think I got it figured out how we can bait those gunmen or whatever they are, right down into town where we can nail them." Doc picked up the dodger and made a little clucking sound. " Such a blasted waste. Did you see how young he was?"

Sheriff Cartland ignored the question to say, " Doc, stick to rolling pills and splinting busted arms of kids which have fallen out of apple trees, and leave my work for me to do."

Bannon was not the least bit perturbed. He put down the dodger and turned towards the irritated lawman " Would you be interested in knowing about that one you shot, up there last night?" Without awaiting a reply Doc went to a chair and sat down, eased back against the wall and reached under his coat to scratch as he said, " He's got a banner-sort-of tattoo on his upper left arm with the words ' Death before Dishonor' inscribed there. Very appropriate, wouldn't you say, Sheriff? And on the other upper arm there is a name : ' Earl Dougherty '. Does that help you any?"

Cartland snapped his fingers, spun and hastened out to the musty storeroom. When he returned carrying a heavy cardboard box which he dropped atop the desk, he said, " I remember the name and the description of that tattoo. I was lookin' through these posters just the other night, Doc, trying to find something on Dan Brady, and I remember seeing this one on Dougherty because you almost never find a feller who's been tattooed."

While Cartland shuffled papers and blew at the dust which his activity stirred to life around that old cardboard carton, Doc discreetly lighted one of his black cigars and Tom was so engrossed that until he found the dodger he'd been looking for and yanked it out to reread it, he was unaware of the bad smell.

Even so, he did not comment as he passed over the old poster. " Earl Dougherty, Doc, right down to the descriptions of his two tattoos. And he was a member of that same Feldon Gang. I think we're getting somewhere."

Doc puffed, accepted the poster, read it minutely through a cloud of bluish smoke, and when he leaned to toss it back atop the desk he said, " It lists Dougherty, Brady, both dead, and two more members of that band—a man named Curtis Wheeler and the head In'ian, a man named Bert Feldon. Sheriff; we got one planted and shortly now we can plant Dougherty. That leaves the other two—Feldon and Wheeler. Have you looked through that box to see what they look like? My guess is that if you don't know them when they ride up to you next time—you know who else I'll be pumping saltwater into before we box you up and let you down six feet into the ground?"

Tom Cartland had not stopped glancing through the posters and now, as he listened to Doc and kept rummaging, he said, " They'll be here, somewhere. I'll bet sound money on it, Doc, they'll be in this box or the other one out back."

Doc flipped ash on the floor. " What did Pocho say—considering it was me offered to pay him for looking around you'd think he'd have the decency to report to me, wouldn't you? Well . . . ?"

" They headed for the foothills up beyond where the squatters have their homestead," said Tom Cartland, and suddenly stopped rummaging in the dodger-carton and raised his eyes to Doc's face.

Bannon was interested. " What is it?"

" The buckskin horse, Doc. I left the buckskin horse which Dan Brady was riding with the J L K brand on it, up at George Cannon's place in a corral."

" Well, what of that?"

" I just told you damn it. Those two outlaws headed back in that direction. They sure as hell must have seen that horse yesterday—must have seen me working cattle on it, and by gawd mistook me for Dan Brady if they was back in the trees watching us trying to get those spooked darn cattle lined out. *Now* I know why they chased me. They thought sure as hell I was their old partner, Brady. They thought sure as hell I was the feller who took that money-belt and tried to make a run for it with their six thousand dollars!"

Doc was gently bobbing his head and chewing the evil little crooked black cigar. " You are probably plumb right," he averred. " I had no idea you had deductive powers, Sheriff."

" What?"

" Powers to figure crimes like Sherlock Holmes had.

Deductive powers they call them. I had no idea . . ."

Tom stepped clear of the piled desk and looked around for his hat. As he was gently lowering it he said, " You got the time, Doc?"

Bannon indeed had a timepiece and dug it out to consult it. " Two-thirty in the afternoon. Why?"

" That'd be about right," stated the lawman heading for the office door, " by the time I get up into the foothills it ought to be getting along towards dusk. I'd as soon not be seen, riding up through to the Cannon place."

Doc removed his stogie. " Alone? Are you light-headed from that crease? You just read what kind of men you are going up against, didn't you?"

" Yeah, and if Feldon and Wheeler catch the Cannons flat-footed, which they sure as hell could do since the Cannons wouldn't be expecting anything . . ."

" Why would they want to bother with those squatters?" demanded Doctor Bannon. " Even if they find the buckskin horse up there, what is that going to tell them? The Cannons don't know anything do they?"

" No," replied Tom Cartland, reaching for the door-latch. " You and I and the Cannons know that, but those damned outlaws don't know it, Doc, and they've got six thousand reasons for being willing to shoot someone before they discover they've made a mistake." He opened the door, paused in the opening to add one more sentence, then he left in a hurry.

" And I may never get another chance to catch up to those bastards!"

Doctor Bannon arose a little stiffly, chewing on the re-
mains of his smoked-down Mex cigar. He went out into
the sun-bright roadway looking around where the lawman
had disappeared on his way across the rear alley where he
kept his horses, then Doc turned, pitched away the stogie
and went hiking morosely in the direction of Abe Markham's general store. Abe had mentioned something about
the township vigilantes last night. Right at this moment
Doc had no illusions about himself, or anyone else around
town, being the match for a pair of professional outlaw-
renegades. He did not believe Tom Cartland was any match
for two of them either, which was why he hastened in
search of the storekeeper. If Markham was looking for an
excuse to show the sheriff and everyone else how valuable
his damned vigilantes were, this might be that opportunity,
and although Doc had no use for vigilance committees in
general, he had even less use for a murdered sheriff whom
he happened to like very much although wild horses could
never have forced him to make such a mawkish confession.

13

THROUGH THE DUSK

Sheriff Cartland rigged out his speedy black horse again, on the reasonable assumption that if he were again required to run for it, or if he were instead required to go in pursuit of someone, he would have the power and the speed under him to do either.

He acted in no hurry once he got rigged out and astride. In fact, while he normally walked a cold-backed horse for a solid mile before booting one over into a lope, this particular afternoon he walked his horse almost two miles, and by then there were unmistakable indications that evening was close by.

Also, because he knew this countryside well enough, and suspected someone might be watching the open range he was passing across, he did not ride directly towards the Cannon claim. He instead cut almost diagonally across in front of the route he would normally have used to get up there, and for a long while he paralleled the foothills riding westerly.

Once, he saw two riders in the south-westerly distance. They had clearly also seen him. Had in fact spotted him before he had detected them, and now they were sitting their saddles like a pair of stone carvings watching his progress. Finally, either satisfied that he was harmless, or having decided he was just another rangerider, they turned on southward. He guessed them to be a pair of old Hartman's cowboys and when they were tiny in the lower-down distance he forgot about them.

The headache was completely gone. Despite the bandage under his hat, which made the headpiece perch precariously, he felt well enough, but he had no illusions; maybe the crease had not amounted to much, as Doc had informed him it hadn't, but he had still lost blood and that would have kept him from dancing one of those all-night fandangoes—if there had been one to dance.

He did not propose rushing rashly here and there in the night, even though he felt capable enough, and when he decided he and the black horse had covered enough ground as a diversion, he reined up through the first few tiers of standing pines and reversed their course, picking his way slowly and prudently along, not convinced that if he had been spotted by the outlaws they might not have paralleled him through the trees to see if they could determine his course.

But evidently that was not the case because he did not encounter either riders or their recent tracks. He found a few cattle tracks, but not too many of those, either. Even if the range critters had not had sense enough to avoid forests—which most of them did avoid by instinct—patrolling rangeriders would have busted them back down out of the trees; losses to bears and cougars occurred no place else and rangemen knew it.

He halted eventually to alight and pace slowly ahead on foot looking and listening. He was within half a mile of the Cannon homestead's rearmost post-and-rider fence. If this were indeed where those two gun-handy outlaws had gone, looking for the buckskin horse and any information they could extract from the men in whose corral the buckskin horse still was, it would be to Tom Cartland's distinct advantage to be damned awful careful. Maybe he had a skull of pure stone, but maybe next time someone wouldn't crease one up alongside his skull, they might aim lower and more to the centre.

For a while he relied almost entirely on two things, his own ability to see, and the black gelding's ability to scent and hear.

Neither of them produced anything until he was at the westernmost corner of the post-and-rider fence, then a sound of several horses walking through the settling dusk in his direction made him step back and lightly lay a set of bent fingers across the soft nostrils of his black. He did not need any horse-talk right now.

But those grazing horses must not have picked up the black's scent because they curved away and went ambling more northward until, right up along the post-and-rider fence, they decided to amble off in the opposite direction, which suited Sheriff Cartland very well.

He thought about leaving the black tied to a corner post, changed his mind and proceeded on down the fence, eastward in the wake of those loose horses inside the Cannons' pasture, but well to the rear of them.

The " dog " started barking and Tom Cartland halted, listened until he was satisfied what animal that was, then he called it a very uncomplimentary name and decided that wolves had a more acute sense of smell—or maybe the wolf had heard him—than ordinary domestic dogs had, and turned away to lead his horse back up through the nearest stand of trees.

This time when he felt confident no one would find his horse, he tethered the black, loosened his cincha, patted the gelding's powerful rump and turned back in the direction of the distant lampglow which he had been following along the rear pasture fence.

It did not seem that there was anyone at the Cannons' log house. At least after he climbed the fence and tested the wind as he circled far around until he could see the front of the place, without causing that wolf on its chain to go into another of his paroxysms of barking, and did not see a horse out front at the tie-rack, and saw nothing in any other way which might have indicated there might have been someone around the place other than the Cannons.

He waited a long while before deciding to go in closer, and now either the wind had shifted—which was questionable since he could detect no wind at all—or else that confounded chained wolf had picked up some tiny sound as Tom advanced, or perhaps some faint scent, but in any case the wolf suddenly began barking and lunging on his chain as he had done that other time Tom had been out here.

This time the sheriff did not wait, he walked briskly on

around towards the far side of the house where the Cannons had slipped out into the darkness, and waited.

The wolf was beside itself. Each time he hit the end of that old chain Cartland held his breath.

Boot-leather softly scraping over rough wood drove Tom over into a low crouch as he sought a sighting as a burly, massive silhouette detached itself from the darker gloom along the rear of the house, long-barrelled rifle in hand, and slipped ahead in the direction of the wolf.

Sheriff Cartland was satisfied. Without more than a cursory knowledge of how Feldon and Wheeler were built, gleaned from their dodgers, he was convinced they could not possibly be duplicates of old George Cannon, right down to the beard, so he softly said, " George—take it easy, this is Tom Cartland."

For five seconds the massive silhouette did not move a muscle, then a low growl said, " Wolf, confound you, shut up so I can hear!"

Clearly, the chained big animal knew exactly what was expected of him when the elder Cannon used that tone to him. He rattled his chain along the log wall heading for his house, dragged the chain inside with him and did not make another sound.

George Cannon said, " Sheriff . . . ?"

" You alone," asked Tom. " I mean—no visitors inside the house?"

" None," replied Cannon, paused, then said, " But we had some visitors. Come over here; I'll leave the back door open. There isn't no light to background you so just slip on inside the house. Me'n the boys'll be watching. Just be quiet is all, Sheriff."

That final admonition would have been unnecessary in any case. Cartland waited a long moment while he satisfied himself there was no one close by, then he started towards the back of the house.

Inside, in the dark kitchen with the smell of a recent meal strong in the air Cartland heard someone ease the door closed after him, then the elder Cannon said, " Follow me, Sheriff," and led the way to the front part of the cabin where two candles were burning in pewter dishes upon a worn old table, and where someone had draped a pair of ancient brown army blankets across both windows.

Cannon motioned. " Sit," he said, and established an example by easing down at a bench across the table from Tom Cartland. " There's a lot goin' on lately," he said in a tone which hinted of complaint.

The lawman asked to be told about the visitors Cannon had mentioned earlier. The answer he got was not what he expected. " Never seen 'em," muttered one of the stalwart younger Cannons as he also came over to hunker at the table, his face long and evilly shadowed by wavery candle-light. " They caught the buckskin horse, dabbed a rope on him and walked round and round him, like they was right interested, then they set him loose, clumb over the back fence where they had a pair of horses tied, and rode up into the hills. That's all of it, Sheriff."

The younger man's father had something to add. " Not quite all of it, son. While you and Alf and Jess was out yonder lookin' at the sign, I used the spyglass to study the uplands and seen a pair of men passin' across that grassy clearing where we shot the old sow-bear last winter. But it's a far piece and all I could make out was one bay horse and one sorrel horse. Couldn't make out the riders at all. They was headin' right on up the slopes deeper through the forest."

"Out of the country, maybe," said Jess, the youngest Cannon.

With personal reasons for not believing the outlaws would leave the country Sheriff Cartland explained how he'd got the head-bandage, how there had been three of those men, and that last night north of town one of them had been shot to death. He did not say he had shot that one because he did not know that he had, although Doc and just about everyone else down around town was convinced that was what had happened. Maybe in time the sheriff would accept this view too, but right now all he said was that during the gunfight in which he was creased, one of those men had been killed, and this made George Cannon peer intently across at Cartland when he said, "Why, Sheriff? What are them men up to? They wouldn't have tried to kill you just for the hell of it. And if they was interested in the buckskin horse—that wasn't no accident either. Do they know that horse from somewhere?"

Tom Cartland went back in memory to what he had previously told the older Cannon about this affair, and added more to the story until he'd brought the Cannons up to date, but he still did not mention the moneybelt nor the money, and this of course left a gap which the elder Cannon detected almost at once, and gazed a trifle sceptically across the table when he said, " Sheriff, if them fellers come all the way over here from around Casa Verde, it don't seem sensible to me they'd do it just to find their partner or his buckskin horse."

Tom relented and explained about the money in the belt under the clothing of Dan Brady. It was no longer much of a secret anyway; not down around Dennison at any rate, and shortly now it would not be a secret out over the countryside either.

He told them about a man named Kildare, even about his letter to the authorities over at Casa Verde, and the last thing he revealed to them was the story of the small-calibre belly-gun found among the effects of the outlaw named Earl Dougherty; the same calibre weapon as the slug Doc had removed from the corpse of Dan Brady.

George Cannon arose without a word to pad over to the stove and fetch back a fistful of dented tin cups and an ancient blue graniteware coffeepot large enough to supply the requirements of a dragoon complement. As he lined up the cups and leaned to pour he said, " Is O'Grady involved do you reckon, Sheriff?"

Tom Cartland was satisfied there was no connection and said so. The elder Cannon acted relieved as he took the big pot back to the stove, then returned to collar one of those full cups as he sat down again. " I wouldn't like the idea of him—a neighbour and all—being part of a murder-gang."

The youngest son said, " I'll tell you something we can

do, Sheriff. We can track them fellers through the mountains if you want us to, and maybe with some luck we can even corral 'em—providin' they don't know we're in behind 'em."

Tom's answer was frank. " It's not your job, Jess, and I don't like the idea of maybe someone else getting shot."

" But the way they was headin' this evening they'll be out of the country in another day or so."

The mighty bearded elder brother said, " Naw, Jess. You just heard him say they come here for that money. Their kind don't give up easy. I know that much about outlaws if I don't know anything else about them."

Tom Cartland could have agreed with that judgement, but instead of confirming it to Jess, he said, " They aren't finished. As for tracking them—don't do it, Jess. Stay clear of them. I'm a little older hand at this sort of thing than you fellers are. It's not that I don't appreciate your offer, it's just that I got my own ideas and systems and other folks buttin' in—even when they mean well—sort of muddy up the water."

Cartland smiled at the younger man but was uncertain whether Jess could make out his expression in that wavery and feeble candlelight.

The older man was concerned about something else. " Will they steal back the buckskin horse? If they tried that, Sheriff, we'd be tempted to buy in. We taken a mighty big shine to that horse."

Tom would have bet new money Feldon and Wheeler did not care one bit about the horse and said so, then he also said, " If you don't have to go up there, stay away. I'd rather you fellers didn't stir them up nor even let them think you know they are out there."

The Cannons looked at each other, then faced Sheriff Cartland again. None of them commented but it was clear they had earlier entertained some idea of becoming involved. Maybe because they did not want to lose the buckskin horse, and maybe their reasons went beyond that.

Tom Cartland arose, drained his coffee cup and set it gently aside. He had accomplished what he had ridden out here to accomplish, and now he had more riding to do in the darkness in order to implement the balance of his scheme.

During the course of his visit to the Cannons he had become convinced that his best course was not to ride back to town and sit complacently awaiting whatever the outlaws decided to attempt; his best course was to assume the initiative and try to get in behind the outlaws, to follow them if possible down out of the mountains, or to attempt an ambush of his own while still up in the mountains, but in any case to carry the challenge to *them,* rather than wait for them to bring the challenge to him.

There would be more peril, quite probably. On the other hand if neither Wheeler nor Feldon suspected they were actually being stalked, the danger might not be as bad as it would become if Wheeler and Feldon saw him stalking them, or picked up his tracks, or in some other way became suspicious.

He thought it was likely that he had the balance of this

night and, with luck, the full day which would arrive after dawn some hours hence, to find those men, observe them, and devise whatever plan might be suitably used against them.

14

A LONG RIDE

When he left the Cannons they stood outside in the darkness silently watching him depart, four large, stalwart men tough as rawhide and as durable as granite.

They knew he was going into the back-country and although he had not confided his rather loose plan to them it required no great amount of perspicacity on their part to guess what he was up to. As Jess said to the others: " I got a feelin' he'll find them, and if he does, him being' alone and all it might not go too well if they see him first."

Jess's father knew his sons; he knew what Jess's comment could lead up to so he said, " We're not supposed to butt in."

Overhead, the sky was filled with bright tiny stars, and if there had been a moon it had departed earlier because now there was no sign of it at all.

Ordinarily this kind of darkness—worse once Tom Cartland left the clearing around the homestead and reached the trees—would have been a very poor time for someone to begin a manhunt.

Cartland had an advantage; darkness or no darkness he knew this back-country as well as he knew the back of his own hand. He had hunted up through it any number of times. He angled to the left a short distance until he found the noisy little creek which came down from the eternally snow-packed lodge-pole peaks at the very spine of the Dennisons, and allowed the black horse to pick its way.

The going was slow and Cartland actually only pushed on as far as the small glade where George Cannon, using his collapsible brass spyglass, had seen those two riders earlier in the day. From this spot he was confident come daylight he'd be able to pick up tracks. Otherwise, this glen was far enough along on his man-trail to give him more advantage after daylight arrived.

He had one blanket aft of the cantle, which was not really enough except that when he hobbled the black and off-saddled him then made up his own bed in the ripgut grass, he did not even remove his boots. He simply lay aside his hat, his holstered Colt and the shellbelt which went with it. Then he rolled into the blanket and briefly listened to the sounds his stomach was making. That coffee down at the Cannon place had been almost pure black acid.

There was some danger of the black horse scenting up those other animals—the bay and the sorrel—and nickering to them. But the longer Cartland waited and listened for that to happen, without it happening, the less he began to believe it ever would happen and he was right. Either there was no scent to be detected or his black horse was too interested in cropping lush grass to be concerned in other animals.

He drowsily decided there could be still a third reason

for his horse to be unconcerned over the possibility of other horses being nearby.

They were *not* nearby.

Just before placing his bandaged head in the only position where the wound did not bother him, he made up his mind that Feldon and Wheeler had not halted after they had crossed this glade, and that meant he would have a lot more man-hunting to do tomorrow than he might otherwise have had to do, if those outlaws had been content to select a nearby campsite.

It crossed his mind just before he dozed off that Feldon and Wheeler had a plan in mind; probably had some idea in mind about going on around through the foothills and perhaps trying to reach the outskirts of town before sunrise in order to be in position down there to begin their search for that laden moneybelt.

If this were so, then Tom Cartland would have been much better off to have remained in town. The trouble was that Cartland nor anyone else possessed a working crystal ball. He yawned, felt the bandage to be sure it was still properly in place, then he loosened his full length and went to sleep.

Once, in the pit of the night an event occurred of which he was blissfully unaware, but had he been awake and had witnessed it his hair would have stood up.

A large rusty-brown wolf with malevolent green eyes appeared upon the fringe of the glade. It circled back and forth, head tipped, nose wrinkling as it tested the air for scents, and the black horse threw up his head, stood stone-still and came right up to the very edge of panic from that strong, gamy smell. Then man-smell weakened the lobo's resolve and in the end he turned to slink back through the westerly forest to go foraging elsewhere.

In the morning as Sheriff Cartland was returning from the creek where he had washed, those wolf-tracks were fresh and about twice the size of any dog-tracks. Cartland zig-zagged around the tree-fringe tracing the wolf's course, and finally, where the tracks hastened off westerly, Tom turned back, looked at his horse drowsing now in new-day sunlight, and shook his head. It ordinarily took no more than a nearby scent of wolves to terrify horses into flight. Even wearing hobbles, an experienced camp-horse could cover an awful lot of ground in record time when he had that variety of motivation to impel him along. But now the black gelding simply opened one eye, watched Tom walk past, closed the eye as though nothing had bothered him in the night, and went back to drowsing.

Breakfast was a frugal affair of one tin of sardines from a saddlepocket, some fresh creek water, and that was all. Then Cartland left the horse at peace and went off on foot to hunt shod-horse sign.

He found it about where he had expected to, if what George Cannon had said about spying two horsemen up here was correct, and clearly it was because the riders had indeed crossed the clearing without stopping and had continued on up-country at the top of the glade where shaggy old pines and an occasional red-fir tree reached up so high they quite effectively cut out most sunlight to the forest floor, and this made reading tracks easier than trying to read them in sunglare.

Cartland became so engrossed in his tracking he almost forgot how much territory he was covering until he came to an eastward opening and found a camp out there.

Here, there was sunlight coming in over the tops of more forest monarchs to reach the ground around a seepage spring where there were no trees and where the still-smouldering embers of a small cooking-fire showed that Tom's arrival had not been more than perhaps an hour late.

He found bay horsehair and sorrel horsehair where two animals had rubbed vigorously, and he also found plenty of boot-marks, but what interested him most was that when the renegades had struck camp instead of heading down out of the foothills they had gone parallel to the open country over in the direction of the stageroad.

He speculated that they might try again to hide their horses and catch a coach on down to Dennison. The main difficulty here was that the morning stage to town did not pass through until about ten o'clock. At least it was scheduled to pass through about ten, but stage schedules in mountainous country were about as unreliable as weather predictions.

Cartland paused to figure. If Feldon and Wheeler did not realise how much of a wait they would have over alongside the roadway, Tom might still be able to overtake them even though he had to now retrace his steps about two miles to reach his own horse again.

If they had perfected a plan for getting down into town

in their hunt for the moneybelt—and the money inside it—they would be reluctant to abandon the plan. At least Tom told himself that as he turned and started jogging back the two miles to his own camp. Human nature did not willingly abandon a plan. At least *his* human nature didn't, and he had to gamble now that the human nature of that pair of renegades would be about the same as his.

The sun climbed steadily. There was an appreciable new-day warmth on all sides, but the forest remained as pale-lighted—in some places downright gloomy—as it usually was, and by the time Cartland reached the clearing where his horse was standing hipshot, switching its tail at an occasional deer-fly, the area was as warm as it would ever be. Very little direct sunlight reached through the spiky tops of all those giant trees.

It probably took Cartland less time to strike camp than it had taken those renegades. Cartland had only one blanket to roll, no frypan to scrub with creekside sand, and no saddlebags to be repacked. He simply saddled up, swung aboard and turned easterly out of the glade, his black horse willing to take long strides as it traced out around the haunch of mountainside upon a faint old game-trail.

Cartland did not own a watch. He, like many rangemen, used his knowledge of the sun's position to make a reasonably close estimate of the time of day, and ordinarily that was close enough.

Maybe it was this morning, too, but Cartland had no way of knowing about this. He *did* know stagecoaches in the Dennison area were notoriously off-schedule nine times out of ten. Of course the morning stage on this particular day, might just ruin everything by being the first coach in weeks to be exactly on time.

But it wasn't. He was a short distance beyond the creekside camp where the outlaws had bedded down last night, on his way across to the vicinity of the coachroad, when he distantly heard the rattle of a large vehicle coming downgrade at a fair clip. Of course, it could have been a freight outfit, except that never in his life had he heard a freight wagon travelling downhill out of a walk.

He angled half a mile uphill, paused to let the horse blow, stood in his stirrups until he had a fair view of the roadway up ahead in the distance—and saw the coach. It was faded red with road-blasted yellow wheels which needed more paint and new tyres.

Turning southward again he pushed the black horse. Then an odd thing happened; three horsemen riding slowly came forth from the forest a mile and more southward, down where the roadway lost most of its pitch and began to settle down into a straight run southward.

Tom strained for a good look at those horsemen, speculating that they might be the Cannons. But they were too far off for him to make a definite identification.

He also wondered if perhaps Wheeler and Feldon had not had an acquaintance down there who might have joined them, making three outlaws not two.

The stage sounded as though it would shake itself apart as it came on down the roadway rocking back and forth on its thoroughbraces, and also listing slightly to left and right.

It took a seasoned passenger to survive a mountain-road trip inside a stagecoach.

Tom urged his horse a little, but as he did so he saw that the whip had boosted his hitch over into a collected little gallop, which was also unusual unless, of course, the whip was a reckless driver, and now the stagecoach began to pick up fresh momentum. Tom was not going to be able to get down alongside the roadway in time. He called the driver a bad name under his breath and tried an angling descent down the slope towards the area where those three riders had been. But even in open country he would not be able to make it in time, not that he especially wanted to catch the coach, he simply wanted to be in sight of it when those outlaws halted it at roadside and climbed on board.

What happened was simply that no outlaws appeared. No one was down along the road. In fact not even those distant three horsemen were still in sight when Tom Cartland pushed ahead in and out among the forest monarchs until he was above the roadway capable of seeing both ways for a considerable distance.

The entire area was now empty except for the coach. Nor did that condition change as the whip sang out to his hitch and rattled past where the lawman was sitting, watching, hurrying southward towards the final upthrust before the roadway settled into an arrow-straight run directly down to Dennison.

Probably, Cartland told himself, those two fugitives had also seen the three horsemen farther southward, and may have thought they could be possemen from town, or at least armed men in search of any strangers at all, subsequent to the shooting of the county law officer.

Whether that was a good guess or not, no one appeared at the edge of the road to halt the stage, so the faded and battered old vehicle went rocking and plunging on ahead without either the whip or gunguard so much as looking at the side of the road.

Cartland swung down to rest his horse's back, hunkered in tree-shade to watch, and by the time the stagecoach was beginning to grow small in the distance, those three riders abruptly appeared again, this time upon the far side of the road and coming directly uphill towards the area where Tom was squatting.

He finally got a look at them and did not recognise a single one of them. One thing he was certain of : they were not the Cannons.

He waited until he could even hear their desultory conversation then decided they were not the renegades either, and that left either rangemen in search of strayed or stolen animals, or travellers passing through without any inkling they were also matters of direct concern to an armed lawman camouflaged by speckled tree-shade over across the road and higher up the slope.

What Cartland deduced was that the outlaws had probably been spooked at sight of those three riders, and instead of flagging down the stage had withdrawn back deeper into the east-side forest to watch and see what the trio of riders was up to.

145

Well, if they were indeed watching, by now they realised that those three horsemen had never been a threat to them.

Tom arose, looked back, looked up and down the side-hill where he was standing, decided the outlaws would either go back deep into the mountains again to camp and rest, and try to halt a coach another time—or else they would retrace their steps until it would be safe to turn southward, and try approaching town overland the way any of the local rangemen would do, no doubt hoping to be mistaken for old Hartman's riders, or the riders from some other nearby cow-outfit.

What all this boiled down to was simply that Sheriff Cartland had been skunked by some innocent horsemen who would probably never even know that through their abrupt appearance up the coachroad they had ruined a lawman's chances of corralling a pair of fugitives, and had also ruined a lawman's personal scheme.

He turned, leading the black horse, and went walking back deeper through the forest in the direction from which he had recently arrived out there overlooking the stageroad.

Somewhere down the hill a mile or more, another horseman was probably walking along beside his renegade partner doing the same thing.

Clearly now, the recourse for Wheeler and Feldon was to lie over until dark when they would not be recognised, would be viewed in Dennison as just another pair of seasonal rangeriders, and make their concerted effort to locate and recapture the moneybelt stuffed with greenbacks; six thousand dollars worth of greenbacks.

Cartland got astride, finally, turned southward and went down through the still and fragrant shadow-world on his way back to town. Odd how things worked out sometimes; a man's best plans turned out not to be worth a damn.

15

A MAN WITH TWO GUNS

He arrived at the shed over across the back alley from his jailhouse shortly past one o'clock in the afternoon, cared for his black horse, stood a few moments along the corral fence watching his two horses, the black and a tough bay gelding, then turned and entered his building, and ten minutes later went out the front door and across to the cafe.

If Wheeler and Feldon were bold enough to head directly for town he doubted very much that they would actually ride down Main Street before dusk.

It was improbable that they realised Sheriff Cartland could have identified each of them by this time, and perhaps except for the fortuitous arrival of that wanted dodger he'd got in the mail he might not have been able to round out all the identifications, but without any doubt the two surviving outlaws had only managed to be free and alive as long as this by being extremely wary. Which probably meant that they would not enter town before dusk when they would be accepted in the weak and failing daylight as just another pair of seasonal rangeriders.

He did not rely entirely on this hunch, but after eating and going back into the warm sunlight of the roadway to make a cursory stroll of both sides of the roadway, he went back to the jailhouse office, locked the roadside door, worked the combination on his safe and removed the moneybelt from its steel-encased place of safekeeping. He took it to the back room and hid it under all those wanted dodgers in their musty old cardboard box.

Maybe that was not the most clever thing he had ever done in his lifetime but Feldon and Wheeler, when they came, would not expect to find their objective under a lot of musty old posters rather than where it should have been, in the office safe.

After that he examined two scatterguns, one an eighteen-inch barrelled, double shotgun, the other also with two barrels but with a much longer, conventional length to it. He placed the short gun on the desk-top and the regulation shotgun over beside the front door.

He considered organising some of the more reliable townsmen, then abandoned that idea because in the dusk a lot of keyed-up individuals walking around with guns in their hands could be a greater source of peril than Feldon and Wheeler could be.

Finally, he went up to Bannon's house to confide in the doctor where he had cached the moneybelt. He did not expect to be killed tonight, but on the other hand those things *did* happen occasionally, and someone else should know where the six thousand dollars had been hidden.

The medical practitioner's reaction to all the sheriff had to tell him was perhaps predictable. He was of the opinion that Cartland should go ask Abe Markham to round up some of his friends. Without mentioning vigilantes that was explicitly what Doc had in mind.

Doc was wasting his breath. Tom had already decided against local participation. With a grunt of disapproval Doc pointed to a chair and after the sheriff had seated himself Doc went to work removing the head bandage as he talked. He wanted to see how well the process of healing was advancing. As he held a lamp close and leaned to see better, he said, " That feller who arrived on the southbound coach this morning was interesting, wasn't he?"

Cartland's retort was not especially enthusiastic. " What feller?"

Doc leaned back and held the lamp to the lawman's face. " That feller . . . Didn't he find you? He told me when we met out front of the stage office he was looking for Sheriff Tom Cartland, so I sent him along to the jailhouse. You mean you weren't in town?"

" Not since yesterday," stated Cartland. " Hurry up and put a fresh bandage up there, will you? I can't sit around here all afternoon."

Doc made no move to comply. " His name was Kildare."

They exchanged a long stare before Cartland repeated it. " Kildare? A Kildare from over at Casa Verde in Arizona?"

" The son, he told me."

Tom faintly frowned. He had only sent off that letter a couple of days ago. " How in hell did one of them get over here so fast, Doc?"

Bannon did not know, for a fact, but he could make a reasonable guess. "It's not China, sonny. If someone had to do it, and was tough enough, they could climb aboard a stage over at Casa Verde and providing they did not lie over at night, they could just about make it to Dennison in something like forty-eight hours, and now that you got me to thinking about it, that young man did in fact look as though he'd been riding a coach that long without any rest . . . Hold still, please."

Doc went to work creating a new bandage.

"He's the other Kildare's son?" asked Cartland. "Did he tell you that?"

"I just told you he said that to me," muttered Bannon. "Maybe this crease alongside the head affected . . . stop wiggling will you!"

Cartland, in the act of instinctively pushing up from the chair, settled back with a mild curse. "Damn it, Doc, get on with it, will you? Where is this feller—at the boarding-house?"

"I would think so, since that's the only place folks can lie over around here . . . Next time we change this bandage you're going to have to get the barber to shave this side of your head." Doc stepped back and put down the lamp after critically examining his handiwork. "Smaller bandage this time, sonny, because the healing is progressing adequately—considering you were shot only last night."

"Night before last, Doc," stated Cartland arising from the chair and looking around for his hat. "I don't think it's *my* memory that's slipping."

The hat fitted much better. In fact it slid down and almost completely covered the new bandage. Tom Cartland halted on his way out and turned to say, " Doc; I'm obliged."

Bannon sniffed. " I got a shed full of gratitude, sonny. You owe me a dollar."

Cartland stared. " For ten minutes and a small bandage —one whole dollar, Doc?"

" You know how long it took me to learn how to patch up wounds like that, and make that neat a bandage?"

Cartland walked on through and out the front door into late-day sunshine. Over in front of the boarding-house a younger man dressed in fawnskin trousers, a white shirt and a pearl-grey Stetson hat was slouching in porch-shade, while elsewhere among the scattered old chairs behind him sat three or four older men looking with mild amusement at the dandified younger man.

Cartland knew instinctively who he was looking at. He saw the pair of ivory-handled sixguns too, worn low and lashed to each leg of the elegant stranger. Cartland groaned aloud, stepped down and strolled in that direction.

The afternoon was advancing now. Up along the distant slopes evening's earliest shadows were firming up in the lower places, and down across the foothills where sunshine still lingered, it was red and rusty-looking.

Approaching town at a light canter from the north-west were four horsemen. Two of them were bearded and all four of them were large, stalwart men, and one of the bearded men who was riding slightly in the lead, was astride a fine-looking buckskin horse.

The elegant stranger leaning upon a porch-upright across the roadway was watching those men; he was especially eyeing the older bearded man riding in on that handsome buckskin, so when Tom Cartland got over there and said who he was, and waited for the elegant stranger to identify himself, the stranger brought his attention around slowly. He had been very interested in that buckskin horse.

He said, " Jack Kildare, Sheriff. I'm from Casa Verde over in Arizona. We got your letter and I came right on over." Instead of offering a hand young Kildare pointed. " You see that bearded farmer or whatever he is, riding in yonder on that buckskin horse?"

Tom turned, recognised the Cannons, and nodded.

Kildare's arm dropped to his side. " That was my father's horse, Sheriff. My father was Jethro L. Kildare of the Indian Wells cow ranch over at Casa Verde. He was ambushed and killed by outlaws on his way back to the ranch after selling off a big herd of our J L K cattle. That buckskin horse, Sheriff, was the animal he was riding the day he was murdered."

Cartland nodded his head. " We figured it was about like that, Mister Kildare. The names of the outlaws were Dougherty and Brady—both dead here in Dennison—and Feldon and Wheeler, still alive and still trying to recover your paw's moneybelt. That buckskin horse was what set me on the right trail. Those men riding in with the whiskery feller on your buckskin are the Cannon family from up in the yonder foothills. Mister Kildare, if you'd come across

153

to my office at the jailhouse I'd be right glad to tell you the entire story."

Young Kildare continued to slouch there in shade watching George Cannon. The four horsemen were near the upper end of town at this time, were in fact hauling down to a steady walk when young Kildare said, " By any chance did those sodbusters have any part in the murder and robbery of my paw, Sheriff?"

" None whatsoever," stated Tom Cartland, beginning to feel a little annoyed towards the elegant younger man with those flashy ivory-handled sixguns. " I'd like for you to come over to my office, Mister Kildare."

The younger man may have detected a rough edge to the sheriff's voice, now, because he studied Cartland a moment, then pulled upright off the post and said, " Lead the way."

When they were upon the opposite plankwalk Cartland asked if young Kildare knew how much money was in that belt. The answer he got was cryptic. " Six thousand dollars in big notes. That was how much the buyers agreed to pay for the herd when my paw took our crew and delivered the herd down at rails-end. That's how much they did pay him, too, because after the murder and robbery was discovered I hunted up the cattle buyers."

" You had some idea they might have been involved?" asked Tom, and got a bold look from the elegantly attired younger man.

" Wouldn't you have?" retorted Kildare. " I didn't believe very many other folks knew about the transaction. But that didn't include some of our riders, and some of the men working at the railroad corrals."

" Another question," murmured Cartland, strolling along slowly. " Did they take anything besides the belt off your paw?"

" The gold watch my mother gave him five years ago on their anniversary, Sheriff. It had his initials inside." When young Kildare paused, eyeing Cartland, the sheriff guessed what was coming and shook his head.

" I don't have it. I did have it, Mister Kildare, but they waylaid me too, and creased my head, then when I came around the watch was gone."

At the jailhouse door Tom paused with his left hand on the latch. " I've got the moneybelt inside, hidden away where I don't expect it could be found very easily. I can turn that over to you but about the watch . . ." He opened the door and turned casually to step through.

Something on his left, over along the south wall behind his desk and slightly to one side of the desk, made a swift, sharp movement. Cartland reacted instinctively, without really thinking; the little steel safe was over there against that south wall. He spun to face that area at the same time his body dropped into a crouch.

Gunfire exploded deafeningly, all of it behind Tom Cartland. He felt the tug of a bullet as it ripped through his shirt low on the right side, but for five seconds he did not heed this because the man over by the little steel safe was swinging his gun-arm to bear. There was a Colt in the man's fist and even while Tom looked the man's thumb-pad

155

snagged back the sixgun-hammer.

That gunfire had made everyone's ears ring. It had also startled the town and aroused it. Men came forth from Shannon's saloon, from the general store, even from the gunsmith's shop and the harness works. A lot of men appeared, but none of them made any effort to walk down to the front of the jailhouse where the gunfire had come from, until four very large, roughly-clad men, two of whom were bearded, shouldered out of the southward livery barn, shoving Brutus Tolbert aside as they started directly northward up the roadway in the direction of the jailhouse.

Cartland knew none of this as he lunged sideways expecting the man with the cocked Colt to fire at him. The man did fire, in fact. The bullet crossed the room and buried itself into one log wall with a solid sound.

Tom completed his draw, but again gunfire exploded in a flurry of incredibly rapid shots. That man who had fired towards Cartland was slammed back to the wall, then he started going sideways until he fell over the little steel safe, rolled off it and sagged on one side in a loose sprawl.

A thin-edged calm voice said, "Are you all right, Sheriff?"

Tom turned. Jack Kildare had both those ivory-stocked Colts in his hands, cocked and riding tilted in case more shooting was required. Tom looked farther, back along the northernmost wall. The other one was over there. He had slid down the wall and was now sitting on the floor over there. He had two wounds which were visible. One directly above his eyes and directly between them, and another wound directly in the centre of his shirtfront where a little spot of scarlet was widening.

Two gunshots from a cold-decked draw in the doorway by a fancy-dan who had no warning at all that when he stepped inside the office he'd be facing a pair of outlaws searching for his father's moneybelt, with each outlaw holding a gun in his hand.

Tom turned slowly back and considered Jack Kildare. He had never in his life seen a man who could draw that swiftly nor shoot that accurately—and not with one hand, but with *both hands*!

Cartland pointed to the sitting corpse. " Pull on that gold chain," he said, " which is draped across that man's shirt."

Young Jack Kildare leathered his weapons, crossed over and obeyed Cartland's injunction. He straightened back holding the dangling gold watch. Without speaking he opened the case, saw his father's initials, looked down at the dead renegade, and finally pocketed the watch as he turned to face Tom Cartland.

" That was just pure damned luck, Sheriff, that we got a chance before they could turn and shoot the pair of us."

Tom considered Kildare. It had not been luck at all, and in fact he had personally never been able to get his sixgun up, cocked and aimed.

Maybe Jack Kildare was a cattleman over around Casa Verde, but in *Dennison* where he was completely unknown, if anyone made the mistake of sneering about those two tied-down ivory-butted sixguns, or those elegant britches and the white shirt . . . Tom said, " If you call it luck, I'll buy that, Mister Kildare, and if you'll sit down I'll go get the moneybelt." He turned towards the door of the back room as Kildare pointed towards the safe.

"It's not in there?"

From the doorway an unsmiling greying-haired individual chewing an unlighted little evil Mex cigar said, "No! It's not in the safe, Mister Kildare."

Doc stepped fully into the office, looked around where the four Cannons were approaching, turned back to gaze at the dead men and say, "Well, Tom, that's Wheeler and Feldon?"

Cartland nodded and went on through into the storeroom.

Doc paused to light his cold cigar, and to look around when the four stalwart big settlers crowded inside, guns in hand. Doc said, "Too late, gents, the killing is over with." Then he jerked a thumb towards young Kildare. "This here is the gent from over in Arizona who owns that buckskin horse you fellers have charge of."

The four big Cannons stood dourly looking from the pair of corpses to the elegant Arizonan. Eventually George Cannon said, "Mister Cartland gone after the moneybelt, has he?" and when Kildare nodded, George then said, "And you got the watch back, did you, Mister Kildare?"

This time the Arizonan did not nod, he simply looked from one Cannon to the others, and finally settled his attention upon old George. "You helped the sheriff, did you?" he asked.

"As much as he'd let us, yes, sir."

"And you don't starve animals nor over-work them?"

"No sir—but we can't buy the buckskin because we just plain don't have any money."

"Keep him for being favourable to the law," said young Kildare, and turned as Tom Cartland strolled back into the office carrying that limp, fat moneybelt.

Doctor Bannon sighed, removed his cigar, stepped back to look outside where a somewhat diffident crowd of curious townsmen were on both sides of the roadway, looking and watching, and Doc beckoned to four of them. "Come in here and help carry a couple of more damned outlaws down by my embalmin' shed, will you, boys?"

No one said much until the corpses had been removed. Then young Kildare carelessly slung his father's moneybelt over a shoulder and offered his hand to Tom Cartland. "Sheriff; any time you're around Casa Verde . . . any time you need a friend in Arizona . . ." He smiled, turned and walked out of the jailhouse heading the direction of the stage company's local way-station. No one said a word and no one stood in his way. But when he was a little beyond earshot Jess Cannon leaned towards Tom Cartland with a comment.

"*Two* guns, and fawn-coloured britches, and a *white shirt*?"

Tom thinly smiled. "He drew against both those outlaws —*and they had guns in their hands, gents!*"

Doc, who was in the doorway, turned. "Like that?" he said. "I've heard of men who could do that but never in all the years I've been around have I believed it could really be done."

"Take my word for it," retorted Tom Cartland. "Doc! you got any more of that Irish coffee up at your place? Right now I could sure use a jolt or two of it."

Bannon briskly nodded his head. "Come along, sonny. I always got a dram or two on hand."

They shouldered through the crowd outside, walking northward in the direction of Doctor Bannon's cottage.